Death and Birth and In Between

Colin Payne

To Simon
Hope you enjoy at least one of these

Colin

Death and Birth and In Between

Cover Photograph by
Tina Payne

Copyright © 2023 Colin Payne

All rights reserved.

ISBN: 9798865049845

Death and Birth and In Between

Acknowledgements and Introduction

BACK IN THE EARLY NOUGHTIES I signed up for a *Diploma in Creative Writing* evening course at the University of East Anglia. I wanted to discover what I was doing wrong. I knew I must be doing something wrong, otherwise why had no publishers accepted, or even responded to, the superb manuscript I had sent them describing my 1997 Interrail train journey from Norwich to Marrakesh. I found it unfathomable that no publisher had snapped it up.

The course was run by the inspirational Anna Garry. My expectation was that I would be focussing on the travelogue, getting ideas on how to improve it. What happened was that the train journey faded into the background and the weekly writing tasks Anna set increased in importance. I enjoyed the course so much that I went back for a second year.

Several of the pieces here originated in that course. For example, one week she brought in a box full of kitchen utensils and asked us to select one and write about it. That gave rise to *Thoughts of a Tin Opener* the first year, and *Ode to a Peppermill* the second. When she asked us to imagine being someone completely different to ourselves, I wrote *Bitch*, and when she brought in a selection of random objects from home, I chose some tiny slippers and, remembering a visit to the old slave market in Marrakesh, wrote *Golden Slippers*.

So, firstly I would like to thank Anna Garry for inspiring me to start writing poetry and short stories.

Once the courses were over, I did intend to continue writing in my spare time, but somehow it never happened. I came to realise that I needed an external prompt, someone to set me homework and a deadline. The first port of call was Norwich's Writers Circle. My first attempt at a sonnet, *Birth*, had its genesis there. Then a few years later, once I had retired, I joined Hilary Mellon's informal creative writing workshops. Many of the pieces here started life in those workshops. The prompt for *The Last Laugh,* for example, was a list of sensory inputs. I chose the sound of laughter and the smell of coffee, and started writing with no idea where the story would end. (Sometimes what I end up writing takes me as much by surprise as my reader.) On one occasion she asked us to write anything containing the word *flat* which eventually gave rise to the song *Krunchy's Final Gig.* I did intend, when I started, to write a poem about a clown who fell 'flat on his face', but I struggled to find a way of incorporating such a non-poetic phrase into the poem. However, I had come to quite like my clown, so persevered and had his jokes falling flat instead. When I read the poem to a friend, he said he liked it as a poem, but thought it might work even better as a song. He was right.

Other prompts, like including a line from a Philip Larkin poem, or making the first line of a favourite poem the last line of mine, or writing about this painting or that woodcut all gave rise to stories or poems that are included here.

So secondly, I would like to thank Hilary Mellon for her inspirational prompts and encouragement, without which this volume would be much slimmer. Also, thanks to all the other participants in Hilary's workshops who have made constructive suggestions over the years.

I would like to thank my daughter Tina Payne who took the cover photograph. The ancient hand in the picture belongs to my mother-in-law, Gigi Hohenthal and was taken in the last minutes of her life. The young hand she is holding is Tina's daughter, Ember, who was a new-born at the time. I cannot think of a more fitting picture for a collection with this title.

A word about the songs: I have been writing songs on and off for most of my life, the first when about 15 years old, before I learned to play any instrument properly. I was given a basic electric keyboard for Xmas which had buttons on one side that generated a few chords. So, without any understanding of how chords worked, I found a sequence I liked and wrote these lyrics to go with it:

Death and Birth and In Between

I was on the train before I showed the pain
And allowed my act to crumble at last
Newspaper opposite raises his eyes a bit
As if to say what the hell are you crying for
Whole years I had had no fears
That the child we had reared had sprung from my seed
And then you told me, staring quite coldly
That the child had never really been mine any way
Behind me I left you crying
And packed up my bags without saying a word
Except goodbye

Immature and pretentious in places, I know, but not bad for a 15-year-old. Please notice that the lyrics tell a story. All the lyrics I have ever written tell a story in one form or another. I am disappointed in so many songs where the lyrics are an afterthought, where rhyme is more important than meaning. I want all my songs to *mean* something.

Some of the lyrics here are autobiographical, such as *Sibelius in the Surf* and *The Bombsite next door,* some protest songs, such as *Catherine Hickman*, and one, *We Don't Mean You*, even a combination of the two. (It is an age-old tradition to use the lyrics of folk songs as a vehicle for protest.) Although some are recent, others are very old, for example *Nobody Sees* I wrote when in my early twenties, and *Song for Leila* was written in the week following my first daughter Leila's birth. She is in her forties now.

I have recorded three albums of songs; the first, *Someone I Used to Be,* was originally recorded back in 1992 with a rerelease planned for 2024, the second *In Aleppo,* was released in 2019, and the third, *Follow Me, is* expected to be released in 2024. They will all be available on good streaming platforms such as Spotify, Apple Music, YouTube etc.

The first edition of *Death and Birth and In Between* was kindle-only and released in 2016, (Amazon hadn't yet started publishing paperbacks). It sold very few copies, and none to people I didn't know.

I would like to thank Jude Wyatt for checking over the manuscript at that time.

I would also like to thank Nick Jackson for looking over all the short stories in this revised edition, pointing out several inconsistencies and suggesting grammatical and structural improvements.

Thanks too to Bernard Perry who similarly looked over all the poems and songs, finding far too many errors. He has also been my *MSWord* consultant, helping me whenever the computer stubbornly refused to do what I wanted.

I am grateful too to Derek and Karen Winterbourne who agreed to proof read the final manuscript.

If any errors did slip through, it is of course my fault alone and not theirs.

Incidentally, during the COVID lockdowns of 2020-21, twenty years after my first foray into creative writing, I finally had time to revisit my Interrail manuscript and, with the benefit of experience gained *en route*, was able to appreciate why no one had been interested. It just wasn't very well written. So I rewrote the book entirely. It was eventually published on Amazon under the title *Steel Wheels to Marrakesh* to very few sales but excellent reviews.

Finally, I would like to say a word about the Notes on page 216. When I initially read out some of these pieces in creative writing workshops, it was not immediately obvious to my listeners what they were about. For example, that *One September Day* is about 9/11, and that *And What Has Time* is about AIDS. So some clarification was needed. I also wanted to enable readers to locate recordings of the songs should they wish to listen. And once I started, I found myself writing notes about more and more of the pieces. Self-indulgent, I know. An asterisk (*) next to the title indicates that there is a note on Pages 216-224.

So, Dear Reader, I do hope that you like at least some of these scribblings, enjoy rather than get annoyed at the twists and occasional voyages into darkness with which some end. If you do, a positive review on Amazon never hurts.

Contents

Across the Fields	*story*	p.1
And What Has Time	*song*	p.6
Archipelago Days	*song*	p.8
Bangkok 1997	*poem*	p.10
Bart	*story*	p.11
Birth	*poem*	p.19
Bitch	*story*	p.20
Catherine Hickman	*song*	p.23
The Cliff	*story*	p.25
Coffee and Cream	*poem*	p.27
The Cruel Incarceration of Pauline Sheldon	*poem*	p.32
Dog's Dinner	*story*	p.34
The Door	*story*	p.43
The Dragon's Breath	*story*	p.48
The Dream	*poem*	p.51
The End of the World	*story*	p.55
Flotsam	*story*	p.57
Fog	*story*	p.59
Follow Me!	*song*	p.62
Fool's Gold	*song*	p.65
For Us	*song*	p.68
Fox Hunting	*poem*	p.70
Gethsemane Again	*poem*	p.71
The Girl on Blades	*story*	p.73
Going Home	*story*	p.76

Golden Slippers	*story*	p.79
Hotel Room	*poem*	p.85
In Aleppo	*song*	p.87
In Broad Daylight	*poem*	p.89
In Neptune's Bed	*song*	p.91
In the Paddock	*poem*	p.95
In the Woods	*story*	p.96
It's Still There	*song*	p.99
Joseph Stanley	*song*	p.102
Just a Slipper	*poem*	p.104
Krunchy's Final Gig	*song*	p.106
The Last Laugh	*story*	p.109
Last Xmas	*story*	p.114
Like a Child	*story*	p.120
Living Alone	*song*	p.132
Lollypop	*poem*	p.131
Mantra	*poem*	p.132
Miss Perkins Takes Ealy Retirement	*poem*	p.135
The Morning After	*song*	p.136
My Dylanesque Song	*song*	p.138
Nobody Sees	*song*	p.141
Not a Love Song	*song*	p.143
Ode to a Peppermill	*poem*	p.144
On Finding a Photograph of the Poet Aged Seventeen	*poem*	p.147
One of Those Parties	*story*	p.151
One September Day	*poem*	p.151
Patchpuddle	*story*	p.154
Penance	*story*	p.156
Playing Ball	*story*	p.159

Reflections No.10	*poem*	p.163
Remembering Douglas	*poem*	p.165
The Returning Sailor	*story*	p.167
The Ring	*poem*	p.169
Ripped	*story*	p.171
A Shaggy Dog Story	*story*	p.172
Sibelius in the Surf	*song*	p.174
Siren	*poem*	p.175
Snow	*poem*	p.177
Someone I Used to Be	*song*	p.179
Song for Leila	*song*	p.182
A Spanish River	*poem*	p.184
The Strand	*song*	p.186
Strangers	*poem*	p.188
Sussex Landscape	*poem*	p.189
Thor's Hammer	*story*	p.190
Thoughts of a Tin Opener on Opening a Tin of Tomato Soup	*poem*	p.197
To Jenny Joseph	*story*	p.198
Tony and the Other Place	*poem*	p.200
Two Sides of the Coin	*song*	p.201
The Violin and the Flute	*story*	p.203
Was it a Murder?	*story*	p.205
We Came from Babylon	*song*	p.209
We Don't Mean You	*song*	p.212
Woman of Shame	*song*	p.215
Notes		p.218
About the Author		p.224
Author's notes		p.224

Death and Birth and In Between

story

*Across the Fields**

THERE IS AN EVENING COMING IN across the fields. She feels it. In her bones. The fields which her father farmed, and his father before him, and his before him. Fields where they walked together every evening. Fields where he showed her how to shoot rabbit with his shotgun and, if they were lucky, the young spotted deer with his rifle. Fields separated from his neighbours by the stream flowing down from the mountains through the forest that they had dammed together, and where they used to catch trout for supper. Fields where she discovered love in the haystack with Johann when just sixteen.

That was fifty years ago now, she realises.

She reflects for a while on how some choices can affect your life so drastically for decades to come, on how things might have been. Sixteen-year-olds shouldn't have to make such important decisions, she thinks. Johann was her neighbour's son and pleaded with her to run away with him. He kneeled in front of her, holding her hands in his, and said he loved her more than life itself. He would die if she didn't go with him. So, in the rush of excitement and passion, she agreed. Even got as far as packing a bag. But once she slowed down, and paused to think about things, she became less certain. It would kill her father, she realised. She also suspected, deep down, that the barriers that divide Johann's community and hers might eventually prove stronger than the love that bound the two of them together. Finally, after days of indecision, she told him, crying uncontrollably, that she had changed her mind. At that moment she saw Johann's love fade from his eyes to be replaced by something different, something colder. He still lives on the neighbouring farm but hasn't spoken to her since that day.

She senses something else following the evening across the fields. Or maybe someone else. Since she lost her eyesight other senses, hearing and smell as well as a kind of intuition, have developed to take its place. She knows they will be coming eventually, with their guns and their knives and their arrogance. To think that, for so many generations, the two communities have lived side-by-side, peaceably.

1

Death and Birth and In Between

The same yet different. The one going to church on Sundays, the other to the mosque on Fridays.

Her father understood. "It's fine when everything works," he told her. "But as soon as something goes wrong and they start looking for someone to blame, they will pick on us." And on another occasion, "You have to work out your escape plan. If possible, have a back-up plan. Maybe more than one. When they do come for you, you will need a way out."

She argued with him. "They are our friends," she said, "our colleagues. We help each other at harvest time, we eat at the same café, we laugh at the same jokes."

He shook his head. "Get everything prepared a long time in advance. Go on helping them at harvest, and eating with them at the café, and laughing at their jokes, and hope that you never need to use your plan. Hope for the best, but prepare for the worst."

The silence in the cottage tells her she is alone now. And her nose. The men who arrived yesterday were drunk, unwashed, and they stank. This morning they left to commandeer another farmhouse in another valley further away. Constantly moving. Anything except actually fighting. Rebels, they call themselves, but she knows they are little better than hoodlums and criminals hiding behind a cause. She suspects that they stole her cow and goat. And the chickens too. Either that or the animals have recognised the futility of her situation and have given up mooing and bleating and clucking in solidarity.

She feels her way to the writing cabinet beside the fireplace. There is a full bowl of fruit on top which she carefully prepared yesterday evening. Her back-up plan. She reaches underneath the cabinet for the hidden catch to the secret compartment. The one with her father's revolver inside. The men took his rifle and the shotgun but didn't find the revolver. That was something, at least. She loads it by feel with her special, homemade bullets. Loads it the way her father taught her to do blindfolded all those years ago when she was, what, just six or seven?

"You never know when you'll have to do this in the dead of night," he said. It isn't the dead of night yet, of course, but for her as good as, and she is glad of the instruction he gave her all those years ago.

Afterwards she stands in front of the window as if staring out at the view, a view that, until ten years ago, she was able to appreciate every day. She remembers how the lane winds its way between the fields and the forest and pictures the tiny bridge where the stream flows under the road. She can clearly remember that day, shortly before his death, when her father led her along the bank of the stream, up through the forest, to the foothills of the mountains beyond.

"The frontier's only five miles away," he told her. "Just the other side of that pass there."

She senses that the shadows are lengthening. She has no sight at all in her left eye nowadays, and minimal sight in her right, just enough to differentiate light from dark.

When her right eye tells her that night has fallen, she walks round the house and checks that the lights are all turned off. Yesterday's wireless told her that it would be cloudy tonight with no moon. So not even starlight. The odds are stacked against her, she realises that, but ten years' experience in finding her way round in the darkness must count for something.

Then she hears it, in the distance. No lorry, not even a jeep or motorcycle. Just the sound of men talking in low voices as they walk across the field. Her field. She smells their cigarettes.

"Just the old woman," one of the voices is saying, "No one else. And she's blind as a bat." She recognises the nasal tones of the village policeman. "The house is dark, so she must be asleep. Or dead – there was talk of rebels hiding out hereabouts somewhere. Maybe they killed her."

"Save us the job." She recognises the second voice. It is deeper and rougher than the last time she heard it, the result of too many cigarettes, but is unmistakeably Johann's voice. For the first time she feels a flutter in her stomach, but not of love – that faded long ago. No, the fluttering is of anticipation,

She opens the cupboard under the stairs, which contains the usual detritus of peasant farmer life: rusty garden tools, an old overall or two, a couple of battered old suitcases, some canes for the beans to climb up, an old broom and broken mop and bucket. She moves the tools to one side and removes the panel from the false wall at the back and quietly climbs through before replacing it behind her. Something else her father gave her. A hidden passage leading beneath the back wall of the house, under the chicken run, to the barn.

She walks down the steps then along, through stagnant water, past a couple of places where rocks have fallen from above. She hears rats scurrying along the tunnel, but they aren't interested in her, they are running past her in the opposite direction. She stops and listens for a moment, wondering what has spooked them, worried that someone has entered the tunnel from the other end, but hears nothing. Eventually she comes to the end of the tunnel. Here her father built steps up to a metal trapdoor. She reaches up and touches the handle but has to snatch her hand back instantly – the trapdoor is scorching hot. She listens and becomes aware, with dismay, of a roaring crackling sound above her. They have set fire to the barn – something her father didn't consider. Her intended escape route is in flames above her. Together with the rucksack containing forged documents she left hidden in the cow pen.

Then she hears shouting from the tunnel behind her – those same voices. They have found the secret panel, not unexpectedly as there was no one to pull the cupboard contents back in place to hide it. The voices are quickly getting closer. Considering her options, she realises there is no choice. She turns and sits on the ground with her back to the wall, facing down the tunnel, gun in hand, with flames above her, rock below and the voices in front of her coming always nearer.

She waits. Suddenly her right eye tells her that they are shining a torch directly at her face. "There you are, you bitch!" the voice shouts. The first words Johann has spoken to her in fifty years.

She pulls the trigger. Six times. Firing her special bullets. The ones that scatter bits of metal in all directions.

The screaming doesn't last long. They die almost instantly.

She walks carefully back along the tunnel. As she climbs over the dead bodies, she hears an echo of Johann's voice from all those years ago. "More than life itself. I'll die if you don't come with me."

When she reaches the cupboard under the stairs she stops and takes another copy of the forged documents from her old gardening overall and puts them in her jacket pocket. Then she picks up one of the old suitcases. Her back-up plan. She stands silently, listening. When she is happy that there is no sound in the farmhouse, she takes one of the canes in her other hand, leaves the cupboard and feels her way back to the writing desk. She runs her hand along the top until it reaches the fruit bowl, which is now empty. Smiling to herself, she walks out of the cottage, careful not to trip over the bodies of the men who had eaten the poisoned fruit, and out into the darkness. Her darkness.

She uses the cane to tap her way along the lane until she reaches the bridge then turns and, following the stream, enters the forest.

song

And What Has Time? *

Life is like a winter flower,
A sudden frost the petals fall.
But which of us can judge our final hour,
And when our curtain's due to fall?

So treasure life it's such a precious thing,
Don't risk it on a pretty smile.
And who's to say if angels really sing
Or, if there's a judgement,
Upwards or down, which way will I ride?

A time in purgatory, a time of fear,
A time to treasure those that I hold dear,
And when the waiting's over,
Then I'll hear my fate.
Oh, won't you tell me,
I want to know,
Who will decide?

> *Why did I go? Why did we play?*
> *I should have known to stay away.*
> *What did I learn? What did I see?*
> *And what has time in store for me?*

And the clock is ticking away,
And the sands run through,
And I still can't decide was it me or you.
And the witness enters the court,
The jury holds its breath.
What she says will determine life or death.

Death and Birth and In Between

So, cherish life, it may be everything,
A newborn baby cries, a church bell rings.
While down here in the dark, canaries sing,
There's life, here at the pit face,
There is hope down here in the gloom.

A broken shield, a rusted spear,
A twisted smile, a wasted tear,
The smell of love, the taste of fear,
Oh no! Who will tell me?
I want to know, who will decide?

Why did I go? Why did we play?
I should have known to stay away.
What did I learn? What did I see?
And what has time in store for me?

And the clock is ticking away,
And the sands run through,
And I still can't decide, was I false or true?
And the jury re-enters the room,
And the verdict's through,
Such a shame, for I still had so much to do.

song

*Archipelago Days**

Waking up to the smell of pine
And the sound of distant waves on a granite beach.
It never gets dark, at least
Not at this time of year,
When starlight is always
Just out of reach.

Laying out the nets
From our old wooden fishing boat.
A family of ducks
Chancing their luck
Dive under the prow as we row.
Our life then was so natural and pure
Just like the water we drew from our well.
Used kerosene lights,
Lit candles at night,
Picked wild blueberries and chanterelles
In a way of life hardly changed
For a hundred years.

> *And we thought that those days would never end.*
> *We'd always wake up to the sun on the waves,*
> *The sailing boats passing in the soft summer haze,*
> *The smell of wood smoke, the log burner blaze,*
> *Those magic afternoons we would mindlessly laze away,*
> *Archipelago days.*

In the evening we'd sit in the sauna
Throwing water on the stones,
And sweat as the waves of steam reached us,
Then we'd jump into the Baltic to cool.

Death and Birth and In Between

And after we'd paint pictures in the fire
As generations have done before,
And maybe we'd grill thick
Sausages on sticks
Which we'd have with sweet mustard
Washed down with beer
In a way of life hardly changed
For a hundred years.

> *And we thought that those days would never end.*
> *We'd always wake up to the sun on the waves,*
> *The sailing boats passing in the soft summer haze,*
> *The smell of wood smoke, the log burner blaze,*
> *Those magic afternoons we would mindlessly laze away,*
> *Archipelago days.*

How could we know that we'd never go back
That it just wouldn't be there for all time
When the boat pulled away
From the shore that last day
I don't know if I even looked behind
At a way of life hardly changed
For a hundred years.

> *And we thought that those days would never end.*
> *We'd always wake up to the sun on the waves,*
> *The sailing boats passing in the soft summer haze,*
> *The smell of wood smoke, the log burner blaze,*
> *Those magic afternoons we would mindlessly laze away,*
> *Archipelago days.*

poem

Bangkok 1997

Traffic fumes choking
Neon Lights blinding
Street urchins smoking
Pickpockets roam
Transvestites dancing
Shopkeepers haggling
Saffron-robed monks
On mobile phones

Traffic cops whirling
White-masked and whistling
Sewer boats surging
Prayer wheels spin
Lunatics mutter
Incense in temples
Dead dog in gutter
City of sin

Limousines crawling
Fat Buddhas smiling
Bar girls are calling
Prostitutes plead
Con men are hustling
Street sellers screaming
Tuktuks are bustling
Society bleeds

story

Bart

IT WAS MY ELEVENTH BIRTHDAY the first time. He came into my room early in the morning when it was still dark, and curled up on the bed by my feet. I noticed him when I tried to move my legs. You know how it is – you shift in your sleep and your legs don't go where you want them to because something is in the way. It was just like that.

I was so excited. I'd always wanted a cat. I already knew his name – Bart, after my favourite TV character. Wasn't it wonderful, I thought, for Mum and Dad to get Bart for me as a birthday present? And so like Mum to let him into my room in the middle of the night as a surprise. I lay there hardly breathing, trying not to move my legs. I didn't want to disturb him. I held my breath and listened for the sound of Mum hiding outside the door, half-expecting her to burst in at any moment, the way she liked to.

Then I sneezed.

And then, of course, I remembered.

Some mornings it happened straight away, the moment I broke surface. On other days it took a while. Once I even got as far as the breakfast table. But always there was that same dull numbing pain in my head when I realised, and my whole world had to be redrawn in different colours.

I knew then that Mum couldn't possibly be hiding outside the door.

I turned over and tried to slide back into the carefree dream world where I still had a mother. But it didn't work. It never worked any more. So, I just lay there waiting for the sound of the milkman on the gravel, sneezing every few seconds, and hoping that it wasn't one of those morning when I would need the inhaler.

Just before dawn I felt the pressure on my legs ease. I lay still for a minute or two, hoping it would come back, but it didn't. When I got out of bed and turned on the light, there was no sign of Bart at all.

* * *

"Happy Birthday, Hal!" roared Dad as the door burst open and he charged in, arms full of presents. He was bigger and jollier and louder than usual, as if trying to be both parents at once.

I unwrapped the presents quickly. First there were two new games for my Nintendo. Then a book everyone had been going on about at school, about a boy wizard. The last present was large and flat. I unwrapped it slowly. It was a photograph of a plump middle-aged woman with blonde hair and the most wonderful smile in the world.

"You didn't have a picture of her," Dad said, and reached over to give my shoulder a squeeze. He swallowed hard. "We'll put it over there, shall we, on the wardrobe?"

"Where's Bart?" I asked at breakfast.

"Who?"

"Bart. My new cat."

Dad put down his coffee mug and turned to me. "I thought about getting you a cat," he said. "I know how much you want one. But with all your allergies I just didn't think it would be a good idea at the moment. The doctor said they'll probably go as quickly as they came once you get used..." He paused for a moment and looked away. "Maybe next year, Hal."

"But he came into my room this morning," I said. "He was lying on the bed. Honestly Dad. I felt him on my legs."

Dad just looked at me and smiled. But the smile wasn't right somehow. It was the smile grown-ups use when something's wrong but they don't want to be too obvious about it.

"We don't have a cat, Hal. I just told you. I didn't get you one. Maybe next year if you're better by then."

I didn't mention Bart again. Not ever.

*　*　*

He returned the next night, again creeping onto my bed in the dark, silent and invisible. I moved my head slowly and opened one eye, but I couldn't see anything. And when dawn came, and the first rays of light started seeping through the gap between the curtains, I felt him leave again.

I was annoyed. I wanted Bart to be a real cat. One that played and purred and chased its tail. One I could feed and stroke and tell things to. I didn't want an imaginary cat. Because I was sure now that was what Bart was.

Back in First School there had been a boy called Darren who had spots and smelt and kept weeing himself. No one wanted to play with Darren, so he invented a friend called Arnold, and played with him instead. It was fine until one day he made the mistake of asking his Mum to pass Arnold the ketchup. After that the teachers used to look at him oddly, and he had to go every Tuesday to see a woman doctor and tell her all about Arnold. It took about six Tuesdays before he worked out what he had to do. He stood up in class one day and told us all that Arnold had gone away and wouldn't be playing with us anymore.

We didn't believe him of course. We knew Arnold hadn't really gone away. Darren went on playing with him as he had always done. He just never mentioned him anymore. It was easier that way.

The more I thought about it, the more certain I became that the same thing was happening with Bart. The difference was that I didn't want a cat like that. I didn't want to be woken up every night by this invisible guest who made no noise and did nothing except lay on my legs.

* * *

The following night, when Dad had finished reading me his normal bedtime story, and had gone through the usual ritual he likes to do, with pulling the sheets up to my chin, and the hot chocolate, and the kiss on my forehead, I stopped him as he was on his way out of the door.

"I want it closed tonight," I said.

He turned and looked surprised. "Are you sure? You always like to have it open, with the hall light on. Are you sure you won't be frightened?"

"I'm eleven now," I said.

After he left, I got out of bed and closed the window. Dad had only left it open a crack, to keep the air fresh, he always said. But I closed it right up and locked it.

If Bart's an imaginary cat, I thought, then he won't be able to get in if I know the door and windows are closed. All I need to do is imagine him on the other side of the door, and he'll have to stay there. So that's what I did. As I was laying there, waiting to fall asleep, I thought with all my might of Bart sitting outside on the landing, unable to get into my room.

It didn't do any good, of course. He came and lay on my legs as usual. Doors and windows didn't seem to bother him at all.

* * *

A few nights later I had a dream. The big old wardrobe in the corner, the one that now had Mum's picture on top, swung forward revealing a secret door in the wall behind. There was a staircase down behind the door and, as I watched. animals started coming up the stairs through the door and into the room, in twos like with Noah's ark. There were cats and dogs and mice and horses and then some strange animals I had only ever seen in books. My room was quickly filling up, and they all came over and sat on my bed, and on top of me, until there was no room left, and I started shouting out, calling for someone to get me out from underneath all these animals.

I woke up to find Mum sitting beside me smiling sadly. She took me by the hand and led me to the secret door and pointed. Her lips parted and for a moment I thought she was going to say something. But then she closed them again and turned her head away, looking back down the staircase, as if waiting for something to come up the stairs.

Then I woke up again, this time properly, and Dad was there looking worried, his hand on my forehead.

"I think you're all right now," he said. "There's nothing to be frightened about. It was just a dream."

I nodded. But I knew he was wrong. It had been more than 'just a dream'.

* * *

Death and Birth and In Between

The following morning I looked at the wardrobe carefully. It was carved from old wood, huge and solid with a massive mirror on the front. I tried to pull it away from the wall, but it was far too heavy, of course. There was something about the wardrobe that worried me now. It was as if the dream had cast a shadow over it. I didn't expect there to be a secret staircase behind. But something wasn't right.

That afternoon when I got back from school, I went to the garden shed and took Dad's bicycle lamp and hid it under my pillow. I decided not to tell him about it. Grown-ups always ask difficult questions, and he would want to know why I needed it. I didn't feel ready to talk about things yet.

Bart came again that night, When I felt him jump onto the bed and curl up by my feet as usual, I reached under the pillow, pulled out the torch, and shone it at the spot at the bottom of the bed where I could feel his weight.

And here's the strange thing. There was nothing there. No, that's not strictly true. Although there was nothing on the bed itself, the torchlight reflected in the big mirror on the wardrobe. And in the reflection, there *was* something there, curled up on the bed, exactly where I could feel it. A large ginger cat, looking just as I had imagined him. The light startled the cat in the mirror, and it quickly jumped down from the bed. At the same time, I felt the weight on my legs ease. But I couldn't see him. Only his reflection, in the torchlight.

"Are ghosts bad?" I asked Dad at breakfast.

"No, Hal, I don't think so," he said absently, reading his letters. Then he stopped and looked at me. "Why?"

"It's for something I'm doing at school," I said. That was always a safe answer.

He looked relieved. "I'm not sure I believe in ghosts," he said. "But if they do exist, I think they must be people who have died and are on their way to heaven but have got a bit lost on the way."

"Can there be ghosts of animals as well?" I asked.

"I don't know Hal. I don't see why not." Then he smiled at me. "I know many people in the village think our house is haunted," he said, "but that's just because it's so old. There aren't many houses that date back to the civil war." He reached over and squeezed my hand. It isn't haunted, Hal. There aren't any ghosts here. You don't need to worry."

I ate my Weetabix and said nothing.

* * *

Bart was a regular visitor all through the winter. He didn't come every night, just once or twice a week. After seeing him in the mirror I gave up trying to keep him out. After all, he was real in his own way. I got used to him and stopped noticing when he came and went. His visits were normal now, not unusual, and I soon learned to accept them as part of my new life, life after Mum, as I thought of it. But I still didn't tell Dad. It would only make him worry. He had enough on his plate. It was my secret.

It went on like that till the summer when Dad finally decided we could afford to have a shower room put in, connecting to my bedroom. The doorway was going to be where the old wardrobe was. When the builders came, they stood looking at it, shaking their heads. Dad wouldn't let them damage it, that was the problem. He wanted it moved over to the other wall in one piece.

"It's a bit of history, that wardrobe," he told them. "It's almost as old as the house. I can't let you break it up."

It took them a whole day to shift it – it was so ancient and heavy, you see, and didn't want to move. It seemed to be holding on to the house, gripping the floor and the walls, determined to stay put, determined to hide its secret a while longer. But eventually the builders won.

When it was out of the way and I was able to look behind it for the first time, I was relieved to see that there wasn't a door there, just some old yellow panelling.

The following evening one of the builders came through as we were having dinner. He had been removing the panels.

"You best come and have a look at this," he said to Dad. "There's a kind of compartment. Have you got a torch?"

Dad went and fetched his torch, and we took turns to look inside.

Death and Birth and In Between

The compartment was about the size of our fridge. Inside there was something white on the floorboards, something which gleamed in the torchlight.

"What on earth do you think it is?" Dad said.

"I've heard about that sort of thing, but I've never seen it before," the builder said.

"What do you mean?" Dad asked. "What sort of thing?"

"They used to bury cats in the walls of houses or under the floors when they built them. For good luck." he said. "It looks like this one was still alive too. Look! You can see where the poor blighter scratched the inside of the panel trying to…"

He was interrupted by the sound of my sneezing. Dad pulled me away, then rushed off to get the inhaler, just in case.

"It must have been the dust," he said. "I was stupid to let you poke your head in there. I should have known better." He thought for a while. "I'll sort it all out in the morning, Hal," he said. "Do you want to sleep in my room tonight while that…that thing is there?"

But I shook my head. I suddenly knew what I had to do and felt sure Dad would be happier if I didn't tell him about it.

"No, I'll be fine, Dad, honest," I said. "I'm feeling better already."

* * *

That night I waited until I could hear the sound of his snoring through the door. Then I quietly got out of bed and put on my dressing gown. I tiptoed down the stairs, careful to avoid the one that squeaks halfway down, opened the back door, and crept to the bottom of the garden. There was a full moon, so it was easy to see where I was going. I took a shovel from the shed and walked to where the earth was soft near the big old tree with the swing on. Then I started digging. It took half an hour before the hole was deep enough.

I went back to the house and, after checking that Dad was still asleep, crawled into the compartment and carefully collected all the bones in an old towel. I didn't sneeze once. I carried them down and laid them in the bottom of the hole.

Then I picked up the shovel again and threw a load of earth onto the bones. But I stopped. Something still wasn't right. I could feel Bart between my legs, rubbing up against them, first one leg, then the other. He seemed to want something. Something more.

Then it came to me. It was strange, and I still don't understand how I knew what he wanted, I just did. I went back to my bedroom and reached under the bed for my old, worn slippers. I took them down to the tree and put them in the hole next to the skeleton. Then, feeling rather silly, and worried in case Dad should wake up and ask awkward questions, I quickly took the spade and filled the hole in again.

* * *

From that day onwards things have got better. When I wake up in the mornings, it's no longer quite so painful to remember. It still hurts, of course, but it's a gentle ache nowadays, rather than that crushing pain I used to feel. I have stopped sneezing too, just as the doctor said I would, and I don't think I'll be needing the inhaler anymore.

And of course, Bart has stopped visiting me. It was only to be expected. He knew where he was going now, you see. He knew the way to heaven and wasn't lost any more.

*Birth**

Emerging from the human tunnel's ageless night ...
Push down, Miss Jones, he's coming. Try to concentrate
And breathe the way we showed you, you've not long to wait
Now ... then detached, an individual knowing light,
Submerged in noise. and bruised by colours, vague but bright,
I breathed and cried ... *At last, it's time to celebrate!*
Well, what a pair of lungs, Miss Jones, they do create
A ruckus. Look, his tiny fist is clenched so tight!
Quick, something's wrong! Where's Doctor!? Bring the oxygen!
And take the child away! I think we're losing her!

Then, at that instant, new-born, frail, I felt the breath
Of ice upon my soul, and watched the angel sent
To lay me on my mother's bosom, falsely tear
Her from me, smile, and whisper that I caused her death.

story

Bitch

THE USUAL FEELING after a night out: head like it's filled with sawdust, mouth like the Sahara, headache like a pneumatic drill.

Try to open my eyes. Only the right one works. The other stays shut. With that dull but all too familiar ache that tells me it'll be a shiner. Must have got into a fight again. My hand reaches up towards it, and finds a swollen puffed-up ball that emits a sharp stabbing bolt of pain when touched.

Wait. Wait. It always comes back eventually.

Open the right eye again. An artex ceiling in tasteless swirls stares down at me, surrounding an ugly pink light fitment with climbing roses. A woman's light. I smile to myself. I wonder whose room this is.

Slowly, slowly. It'll come back soon. Patience.

A fragment, That Goth in the pub. Foreign. Slapped me when I touched her up. Bitch. Must be a lesbian. So I slapped her back. Hard. Floored her. After all, can't have that, can I? Not in front of the others.

Must have been out on a long one with the lads. We've had a lot of those recently. Wonder what the fight was about. Wonder which of the girls I managed to fuck this time.

It wasn't the Goth, that much I can remember. She just did that thing with her eyes till all you could see were the whites, and started mumbling in foreign, then left. No matter. Weird Bitch!

Damn! Come on! Come on! Why is it I can remember some things, but not others? I remember slapping that Goth, but not where I was or who I was with. And when I try to focus on the lads, they fade away into the mist.

No matter, I'm in bed with someone – might as well find out who.

My left hand slides under the covers slowly outwards until it reaches the edge of the bed. Then back again. A deep breath. Now it's my right hand's turn. Slowly across the sheet until it reaches something soft and warm. I smile to myself. Slowly, slowly, almost imperceptibly, my hand rises upwards until it reaches the hollow between two shoulder blades. My smile broadens. Even if I can't remember much about last night, I can at least enjoy the morning. With gentle movements I run my fingertips around in small circles on the soft skin.

A voice from the pillow next to me moans gently in sleep. My hand stops its explorations. Something's not right. Hanging in mid-air my fingertips wait, poised, and the breath that was just about to leave my lungs changes its mind and stays there. There it is, the voice again.

"Hmmm...yes...yes..." It is a soft voice. A gentle voice. But unmistakably, it is the voice of a man.

Slowly the smile fades from my lips. Christ! How drunk was I? Eyes closed again I lay back on the pillow in the early morning silence, unmoving, exploring backwards with my brain, trying to work out who...and where... But it's still gone.

God, it's taking its time to come back this time.

I slide very slowly off the bed, making sure that the covers don't move, trying, willing, the person next to me not to awaken. Now I am on the floor. Through my one good eye I look for my clothes, but can see only women's stuff – bra, panties, high heels, and a torn blouse with something red on the front, wine maybe. Or blood. Damn! But no time to worry about that now.

Tiptoeing round the bed, I find some trousers and a shirt on the floor. They too are unfamiliar. But I'm past caring now. I just want out. Home, wherever that might be. I take the trousers and shirt in one hand and creep slowly, so slowly, towards the door.

It's never taken this long to come back before. Jesus! Come on now! Come on! I can't even remember my name. Must have been a hell of a party. But, Christ! In bed with a man? I wonder what I ... I mean is it possible that I ... Jesus! How will I explain this to the lads?

The door opens onto the corridor. The figure in the bed is breathing deeply again. Not quite a snore, but not too far from it either. I close the door behind me and creep along the corridor.

The first door I open is in the semi-dark, curtains drawn, lit only by the glow of a nightlight. A child's room. I hear a young voice mumbling from behind a dream, "Mummy...mummy..." Then a muffled sound, like sobbing. Something inside me makes me want to move over, and hold the child in my arms. But I shake my head and close the door behind me. No time for that shit.

The next room is a bathroom. I slip inside and close the door behind me. Just need a moment to throw the clothes on and examine the damage to my eye.

I pull the light cord and move to the mirror. Staring back at me is one of the most spectacular black eyes I have ever seen. But it's not that that grabs my attention. It's the rest of it all. The other eye is blue, and bears the unmistakable signs of smudged mascara and eye shadow. It blinks back at me in disbelief. Surrounding them is a head of frizzy, unnaturally blonde, but definitely feminine shoulder-length hair.

The face now has an expression of panic mixed with pleading, as if the mirror is the window out of some prison and it is hoping to escape.

The good eye closes and my hands, which have made their way to my throat, slowly start to move down my body. But I know, somehow, even before they reach the, definitely artificial, 36DD breasts, that something very strange is going on.

Suddenly the door bursts open and the figure from the bed is standing in the doorway.

"What the fuck are you doing with my wallet?" he says.

The same voice as earlier, but not gentle any more. Far from it.

"And who told you you could get out of bed? Bitch!!"

He grabs my hair and slams my head against the tiled wall. And as I begin to slide into unconsciousness, I can feel him hauling me, still by the hair, back towards the bedroom.

song

Catherine Hickman*

Catherine Hickman worked from her home
Making dresses each day by her window.
Her eleventh floor flat in Lakanal House
Enjoying the view over Camberwell.

One day while sewing she noticed some smoke
Rising up from a flat down below.
Without thinking twice, she dialled 999
And asked what they thought she should do.

> *"Stay put!" said the operator, "We know where you are.*
> *Someone is coming, you won't wait for long."*
> *"Stay put!" said the operator, "You're best where you are,*
> *I'll stay on the line."*

Catherine was an obedient soul,
She respected authority, did what she was told.
She stayed in her home, though her instinct said flee,
The operator was holding, you see.

"Now there's smoke through the floorboards,
What shall I do?
Shall I go to the stairs, try to make my way through?"
Catherine was waiting for that fireman to come,
But Catherine waited in vain.

> *"Stay put!" said the operator, "Don't open that door!*
> *You don't know what's out there, and neither do I."*
> *"Stay put!" said operator, "Best stay where you are,*
> *I'm still on the line.*

"But it's getting so smoky in here,
And it's getting so hot,
And it's getting so hard to breathe,

Death and Birth and In Between

    Oh my God! The curtains are burning!
    Oh my God! There are flames at the door!
    Oh my God! It's orange, orange everywhere!"
    Then the ceiling came down.

"Hello Catherine," the operator said,
"Catherine, are you there?
Catherine, can you hear me?
I think we've lost the line."

    On the phone for an hour
    To the emergency operator,
    Why could nobody save her?
    Dear God! Why didn't they tell her to run?
    Dear God! Why couldn't that fireman come?
    Dear God! Why did they use that cladding that burned?
    Who's to blame?

Her sisters said they hoped that lessons were learned,
Changes would be made before more people burned.
Her sisters prayed it wouldn't happen again,
That Catherine did not die in vain.

Seven years later another fire,
Seventy-two people died this time in Grenfell Tower.
Firemen told people to stay in their homes,
Some survived because they disobeyed.

No lessons were learned from Lakanal house,
They still used that cladding that helps flames to rise,
That turn high-rise blocks into tombs in the sky,
Made of shoddy materials, but kind on the eye,

Won't retrofit sprinklers so no one need die
Won't sacrifice profit to save human lives
So sad, but it seems Catherine Hickman died
In vain.

story

The Cliff

I DECIDED AGAINST THROWING myself off the cliff in the end – I just didn't have the bottle. Great in principle, but the actual act of jumping was too hard. I did try a run-up, but then screeched to a halt just before reaching the edge and found myself terrified of falling off, which doesn't make sense I know.

The thing is, I don't like pain. And I suspected that jumping off the cliff might hurt. Not the jumping bit. But the landing. At least for a moment.

Instead, I decided to go down to the beach and just walk out into the water until it covered my head. So I waded in, got in up to my knees, but I'd clearly chosen the wrong time of year. I was in so much pain from the cold I had to give up.

There must be an easier way. I thought.

I decided to climb round the boulders at the base of the cliff till I found a really deep spot then just jump in – surely that should work without hurting too much?

***

I had thought that deciding to top myself would be the difficult bit. Once the decision was made, doing it would be easy. But it wasn't like that.

It hadn't been that hard to make the decision. There wasn't a single good thing in my life any more. Hadn't been since Dad died. He was always the one who played with me and gave me his time. We used to go for a walk every Sunday morning along the cliffs. He used to ask me things and actually listened to my answers.

One thing he told me was this. "If anyone picks on you, it's because they think you're weak. You've got to show them you're not. Don't start it. But if they hit you, hit them back harder. You may lose the fight, but they're less likely to pick on you again once they know you can fight back."

Death and Birth and In Between

Then he bloody died. And there was just me and Mum. Mum, well, I don't think she really likes me, to be honest. I don't get on with her new boyfriend either, and when he's around she forgets I exist. Sometimes she even forgets to cook me dinner.

But what really clinched it was when an older kid started picking on me at school. "Tommy no friends" he called me, which was true enough I suppose. One day he pushed me over, showing off to his mates. So I got back up and hit him. I remembered what Dad had said. Floored him. I got hauled up in front of the Head and they called my Mum in.

"Fighting!" she said afterwards. "Whatever would your father have thought?"

I tried to tell her what Dad would have thought, but she wouldn't listen. She took away my phone and iPad for a whole month. Yes I know I knocked one of his teeth out, though I'm sure it must have been loose beforehand. But he started it. He hit me first.

I just didn't see the point of going on after that, and couldn't see how things were ever going to get any better.

***

I had just started moving towards some boulders at the bottom of the cliffs where there was a nice deep pool when a family came down the track – a woman and her two sons. Very inconvenient. I sat and waited for them to decide it was too cold and leave. It wasn't really beach weather. But no. Instead, they started picking up some pebbles and whacking them with a hammer and chisel. Bonkers.

They did seem very excited about what they were doing though so, after a few minutes I strolled over to see what was going on. After all, the pool wasn't going anywhere.

One of the boys, the one with the ginger hair, was about the same age as me.

"What are you doing?" I asked him.

He smiled and beckoned me over to have a look.

It was strange – inside each of the pebbles was a weird spiral thingy like some sort of shellfish.

"How long have they been there?" I asked.

"Millions of years," he said.

"180 million years," his mother added.

"Is that when the dinosaurs lived?"

"Older, I think," she said. "The dinosaurs didn't become extinct until 66 million years ago."

How about that!

"They're called fossils," Ginger told me.

Fossil. That was what we called our old geography teacher, the one with bad breath whose teeth kept falling out when he spoke. I'd never understood his nickname before.

"Do all the pebbles have these things in?" I asked.

"No, but on this beach lots do. And there are other things too. Look, here is a fish skeleton, and here is a kind of prehistoric squid we found earlier." He handed me his hammer. "You have a go." he said.

So I did! And it was so exciting – you just whack the pebble and it splits down the middle and there's this creature curled up inside. So I did another one. And another. Sometimes it split with just the hammer. Sometimes you needed a chisel too.

When it started getting dark, we walked back up the path to the road together. Ginger asked me to come down with him the following Sunday.

"Mum won't let me come down on my own, but if there are two of us, it should be ok." And then, "By the way, why were you on the beach in the first place? We only ever see fossil hunters and beach bums down there."

But I didn't answer – it no longer seemed important.

poem

*Coffee and Cream**

Part 1
the cracked and tarnished station mirror
considers the reflection of my
tarnished and cracked grime-encrusted skin
('black as sin,' they said)
before turning away in disappointment
judging me guilty

guilty of allowing once sparkling blue-grey eyes
('how strange for a blackie,' they said)
to turn dull and fearful
like a whippet
kicked for daring to beg
at his master's table
or a galley slave
waiting for the overseer's lash
to turn his sweaty black back red

guilty of stealing a rose virgin white
from a suburban garden
('it's against God's natural order,' they said)
to adorn the torn lapel
of a pawn shop suit
that also didn't know its place

guilty of creeping away
bloodied and bruised
one autumn morning long ago
tail between legs like that whippet
('keep your filthy black hands off our women,' they said
with their boots and their clubs)
before the dawn chorus
could announce my cowardice
in discordant harmony

Death and Birth and In Between

Part 2
in my pocket a crumpled page torn
from newspaper once destined
to patch my sole
studied in my high-street-lamp-lit
shop doorway bedroom
words jumbling and jumping and blurring
on the page
meanings hidden until
kicked in the stomach yet again
by the eventual revelation
peering remembering weeping
peering once more
how can I now mend my soul?
how can I now atone?
Elsie, oh Elsie
my Norfolk rose

Part 3
the train journey familiar yet strange
track still hugging the river bank
steam and smoke no longer seeping
through gaps around the window
like an unwelcome outsider
wrinkled noses still averting their gaze
(keeping their distance just in case)
even the ticket collector with his
fearsome clipper and
bird beak peak
looks away

once I was prey
how now do I dare return?

the river flows like time
onward always onward
three passing wherries avert their gaze
in embarrassment while nonchalantly

examining reeds on the opposite bank
sensing my shame

a lifetime ago we made careless love
in those soggy reeds observed only
or so we thought
by a solitary seagull voyeur

too many years since
of water under and trains over
that particular bridge have passed
the age not yet right
for coffee and cream in the same cup
you might say

Part 4
at the graveyard standing apart
invisible still yet in plain sight
beneath a willow weeping
raincoats shuffling
umbrellas sheltering
priest droning
a young man steps forward hesitant
bare-headed in the rain
throws the first handful

suddenly they are gone
to The Lover's Rest maybe
for sausage rolls and tepid beer
and bitter coffee and awkward silences
and quick escapes

shuffling to the open grave I hear
her calling me as always
(or is it the seagull's voice I hear?)
reaching to my lapel I throw in the stolen rose
before turning my back on her
yet again

Part 5
the young man appears unnoticed at my shoulder
blushing, "are you...?"
stammering, "did you...?"
mumbling, "...Elsie, my mother?"
his nose not wrinkled
his gaze not averted
his eyes not judging
his voice not accusing
his skin not white but neither black

suddenly I see him
see her through him
recognise her nose and lips
recognise too those once familiar
sparkling blue-grey eyes

"are you coming? we have
sandwiches ... cakes ... tea ...?"
I follow but know now
that it is far too late in the day
for coffee and cream

poem

*The Cruel Incarceration of Pauline Sheldon**

Down here beside the old wine store
The darkness like a cloak around
Me gathers, there is ne'er a sound
As I, neglected, wander round
My gaol beneath the kitchen floor.

Too well know I these ancient beams,
These cobwebbed curtains undisturbed.
Too long this maid, undone, deserted
By her lover, sits and stirs
Her cauldron full of baffled dreams.

Here on love's perjured cold stone bed
Unseeing and unceasing must
The hands of time sweep on, the dust
Of lifetimes settling, sealing up
The place where once this maiden bled.

One corner of my cursed home
I do eschew, the place where last
Did beat this devastated heart
Where I emaciated starved
And where now lie my yellowed bones.

A sound of movement up above!
In haste I scramble to my feet,
My soul has not embraced defeat
Yet. Has he come to set me free?
The jewel of my life, my love?

Death and Birth and In Between

Yes! What was that? Rats' feet I'm sure!
I struggle to the steps and climbing
To the top, I wail and cry
And hammer on the hatch, "It's time!!
Oh God! Help! I can take no more!"

But no one comes, although they hear
Me, none know how to set me free,
Because I'm one who weeps unseen,
Imprisoned long ago, believed
Not to exist at all. My tears

Were shed before the folk above
Appeared, they were not even born.
There's none alive now can recall
The story of the servant, Pauline
Sheldon, locked away for love.

They never stay too long, the ones
Up there, they move in full of joy
But soon their peace I do destroy
And haunted by the chateau's noises
Few can sleep at night, and some

Time soon they all depart again.
And then, when tranquil, I can breathe
Once more. The crumbling chateau sleeps,
The cellar's silence offers peace
While I my love's return await.

Down here beside the old wine store
The darkness like a cloak around
Me gathers, there is ne'er a sound
As I, abandoned, wander round
My tomb beneath the kitchen floor.

story

Dog's Dinner

Part 1

SHE STIRRED HER TEA SLOWLY. Ten circles to the right, two to the left, tap once on the edge of the teacup. Only then was she happy to put the spoon down in the saucer.

She took a sip and picked a biscuit out of the plate. She always laid out four biscuits, even though she never got through more than two. It was something to hold on to. If she stopped putting the biscuits out, then it was as good as admitting he would never come back, and she couldn't do that. Ever.

It was a rich tea biscuit. It had to be rich tea – George's favourite. She had tried digestives once, but it wasn't the same. She felt disloyal. And anyway, they went soggy when she dipped them in the tea.

She nibbled a small piece from the end.

Whisper watched her from his basket. He was chewing a piece of old wood, an old chair leg, but still had one eye on the biscuit. When most of it was gone, he stood up, stretched, and wagging his stump of a tail, hobbled over to the table and waited.

She took another sip of tea, and a final nibble of biscuit. Then she threw the remainder to the dog who, today as always, caught it deftly in mid-air and swallowed it in one.

She looked at the chewed chair leg and sighed. The butchers used to give away doggy bones, but now they want you to pay. A pound for a decent bone! Why is everything so expensive nowadays? She felt it was something to do with all the foreigners that had moved into Lansdowne Grove in recent years but couldn't put her finger on why.

She turned to the dog. "I'll get a proper bone for you at the weekend, Whisper, I promise!"

She looked at the clock. Five to four. Five more minutes and it would be time for his walkies. It wouldn't do to leave too early. She liked to be closing the front door just as the last of the four o'clock chimes rang out from St. Matthew's. Not that either of them was up to much walking nowadays – the trek to the bench in Lansdowne Park seemed to get longer every day. Only a half a mile, but her hip was in such a state that even with the stick it took a good twenty minutes.

She stood in front of the hall mirror and fixed a headscarf over her hair. It had been a long while since she had been able to afford a visit to the hairdressers, but the headscarf concealed the worst of it. Maybe Indira, the Pakistani woman downstairs, would give her a cheapie. Or was she Indian? She could never remember. She didn't really like going to Indira – the flat always smelt of that strange foreign food they ate, and she found that sari thing that Indira wore so strange – indecent almost.

Part 2

I was young then, and they used to say I was pretty, though I couldn't see it myself. I thought my eyes were too close together. And that front tooth was just a touch crooked.

But the first time I saw him I felt like Rita Hayworth. He looked at me with that half smile of his and his eyes drank me in like I was champagne. I felt he could tell everything I was thinking, just by looking at me.

1947, it was. He had just been de-mobbed and had only been at the hotel for a couple of weeks. He worked on the door and looked so smart in his brown uniform, with that peaked cap and his neat little moustache. My heart did a butterfly turn every time I saw him.

I worked in reception. We had a huge coal fire burning day and night in the winter. He used to come in when things were quiet and talk. He told me stories about the war. His time in Burma. I used to look forward to those times – if he didn't come in, I felt cheated. You know, like when you've waited for your Coronation Street and they cancel it because of the tennis or something.

Then one day it happened.

"Do you dance Mildred?" he asked.

I tried to answer, but the words just tangled up in my throat.

"Finish at five, don't you? Get yourself changed. Best frock. Meet you outside the hotel at eight. We'll go dancing."

And dance we did. That night, the next, and three times the following week. And when he asked me to marry him six months later, well, it was almost as if I'd known him all my life.

But I hadn't known him all my life. And later, when he went away, I realised I didn't really know him at all. He spoke so much, so easily, but in the end, he said so little.

We moved into the small flat in Lansdowne Grove, near the park and opposite St Matthew's. And those two years were the happiest of my life.

But a voice inside my head told me it couldn't last. You don't deserve him, it said. He's handsome and charming, and you're plain and shy, it said. Your eyes are too close together, and your teeth are crooked. It can't last. You're not good enough for him.

And the voice was right. One day when I got back from the hotel, I found his half of the wardrobe empty and one of the two matching red suitcases missing from under the bed.

Nobody would look at me at work the next day. But the letter didn't arrive until eighteen months later.

Part 3

5th January 1951

Dear Mildred,

Well, what can I say old girl? It was a good couple of years, wasn't it? We had that at least. Thought it would last longer. But then I got word from Chalky. You remember him? He was at the wedding. He'd been back, you see. To Burma.

There were some things I never told you about those days. I was ashamed really. It's not easy to admit you're a coward. But I was. When the bullets started flying, and a mate got a bayonet through his guts, I just couldn't take it. Ripped off my helmet, threw down my gun, and ran away. Into the jungle. Don't remember much about it.

Just the insects. There was no way to avoid them, you see. They crawled into my boots and under my clothes and bit me all over and made life hell. And even worse than the insects were the leeches. The itching was unbearable. Worse than any torture the Japs could have put me through.

Then one day I heard some Japs coming through the jungle and decided to just walk up to them and let them finish me off. Whatever they did to me wouldn't be worse than the leeches.

Anyway, I started walking towards them, when out of nowhere this young girl popped up, grabbed me, put her fingers to her lips and led me away to her village.

She was good to me. Hid me. Fed me. Stayed with me. Saved me from the Japs. Saved me from the leeches. Liu-Chi her name was. Whenever the Japs came there was this hole in the ground underneath her hut she would put me in.

Then some British soldiers came. The villagers didn't warn me about them. Meant to be on the same side, you see.

Took me back and locked me up. Said I was a deserter. Shipped me home in irons.

It wasn't till the war was over, they let me out. That was when I started at the hotel and met you. Thought maybe we could make a life together. And it might have worked.

But Chalky went back to the village. He told me that Liu-Chi had a child. A boy. Half white.

My son, Mildred! I had a son! A son I'd never seen. Surely you can understand? I went straight to the docks. Got myself a job on a tramp steamer to Singapore.

He's a strong healthy boy, Mildred. We call him Chacko. It was meant to be Jack, but they can't say it right, so Chacko it is.

I'm going to stay on here with Liu-Chi and Chacko. I don't know how long for, maybe a year or two, maybe longer. I will come back one day, Mildred, I promise. And I'll look for you then. But I can't say when. Don't be too angry with me.

Your
George

Part 4

7th July 1997

Dear George,

Happy Anniversary Darling! Our 50th! That's Golden, isn't it!? Doesn't time fly?

I hope you are well. Whisper and I keep struggling on, though neither of us is as young as we once were.

As you can see from the address, I am still in Lansdowne Grove. I've been here so long now I don't think I could ever move. Mind you, it's not the same as it used to be. Old Mr. Waterford upstairs died last month. Very sad. He's been here as long as us. And when the new people moved in they were foreigners. Nice enough, in their own way, but it's not the same, is it? But that sort of thing is happening all over.

The landlord brought a new bed over last month. You know, all these years I've had the same one we used on our wedding night. But don't worry Darling, the new one is a double as well. So when you get back there'll still be a place for you. There'll always be a place for you. I keep your side of the wardrobe empty, just as you left it.

Oh yes, we got that new freezer the other day, the one I wrote about last month. The thing is, the landlord got the wrong size. It's far too big, and the shop wouldn't take it back. He must have got it cheap in a sale, I suppose. Well, of course, there's no room in the flat for it – you know how small the place is – but he was so nice, he cleared out the cupboard under the stairs and put it there. It's quite safe. I can lock the lid and no-one else can get in.

Whisper's legs are playing him up again, and I suppose I ought to take him to the vet, but they're so expensive I keep putting it off. Maybe we can do it when you come back.

I don't know whether you get these letters of mine. I send them to the consulate in Rangoon, with POST RESTANTE on the cover, and they don't come back, so I suppose you must. Mr Waterford, he told me about this Post Restante system. It's quite clever, isn't it?

I've got to finish now. Whisper knows it's time for his walkies, and I'd hate to disappoint him.

Yours forever,

Mildred.

xxx

Part 5

She recognized him the moment she opened the door. He was older, of course, much older, and the moustache was white. But it was definitely George. His face had accompanied her in dreams every night for the last fifty years.

She opened the door. "Hello Darling," she said.

He looked at her. "Hello Mildred." He stood on the doormat uncertainly. "Can I come in?"

"Of course, George." She smiled. "This is your home. I knew you'd come back."

He stood awkwardly. "I was at the embassy a few weeks ago, you see, getting my passport renewed. They gave me these."

He took a bundle of envelopes from his jacket pocket. Then he reached over and touched her cheek gently.

"I didn't think you would still... After all these years." He shook his head. "Why?"

"What a silly question, George. Don't you remember? Because when you wrote you said you'd come back."

"But that was fifty years ago! Surely...I mean...did you really think..."

"When we married, George, we said for better or for worse. We both took that vow. We were united. One person. You are part of me, George, and always will be." She smiled. "And I was right to wait, wasn't I, George? Because here you are."

He shook his head. "I don't know why I came. Well, yes, I do. I wanted to say..." He stopped. It was strange. Words came so easily to him, but now when he needed them most, he was having trouble finding the right ones. "I wanted to tell you, Mildred...don't wait any longer. I'm not coming back to you...not ever. I shouldn't have come now. It was a mistake."

He stood up and walked to the window. "I live in Burma now, Mildred. I married Liu Chi and have three children and eleven grandchildren."

He stopped. This wasn't coming out the way he had intended. "That is my life now, old girl. The time with you here was, well, just a dream. A nice dream, yes. But no more."

He turned and looked her in the eyes. "You know, I don't think I'd thought of you for forty years, Mildred, until they gave me those letters."

He looked deep into her eyes with sadness, but then, shifted his gaze to her hair. He reached up and touched it gently. "Let yourself go a bit, haven't you, old girl? Looks a bit like a..."

He had been going to say 'dog's dinner', but at that moment Whisper sat up and started growling. Strange. They say dogs understand more than we think.

When he looked back at her, she was still smiling but something had changed behind her eyes. Like a door shutting. He didn't notice.

"You wrote that you had got a new bed. And a new freezer." He laughed and shook his head. "The interesting life you lead."

"Yes," she said. "Come I'll show you."

"No, you don't have to, I mean I'm not really…"

But she was already hobbling out onto the landing. She opened the door to the cupboard under the stairs.

"There it is George." She took the key from her apron pocket and opened the lock. "I've got a gateau at the bottom somewhere George. I've been keeping it for when you come. But I find it so difficult to reach nowadays. Would you mind?" He looked at her sadly, before laughing again.

"Of course not, old girl. Whereabouts is it?" She pointed, and he leant over.

Part 6

When she and Whisper returned from their walk, the following afternoon, her hip was aching more than usual. She closed the door behind her and sat down. She took off her shoes and put on her old worn slippers.

The dog lay down noisily in his basket and started chewing at his bone. She opened a cupboard and pulled out a large casserole dish.

It had been so easy really. One little push, that's all it took. And a twist of the key. But he should have guessed that she couldn't let him go again, not after all this time. Funny. He always used to know everything she was thinking. Not this time though.

Really! And he thought she would let him go back to his darkie whore! Had he forgotten who his real wife was? She smiled to herself. Maybe it's all for the best. This way he really would be a part of her forever.

She turned to the dog, who was still working on his bone, trying to get his tongue in the eye-socket to the soft juicy mush inside.

"Now Whisper, let's see. What shall we have for dinner tonight?

story

The Door

I HAD NEVER NOTICED IT BEFORE, though I must have walked past it on my way home from school dozens of times. It was a drab green colour, about two foot tall, with a brass knocker. It was a door. The wrong size of course, but definitely a door. It was hard to see in some strange way. When I wasn't actually looking at it, it kind of merged into the background, but once my eyes found it again, I could see it clearly.

As on every Wednesday afternoon, I was sent home early when all the other children had football practice. I would have loved to join in of course, but I couldn't. Because of the brace on my left leg. My ankle wasn't strong enough, the doctor said, so I had to wear a brace.

Mum was meant to pick me up on Wednesdays, but she had forgotten.

Again!

So, I walked home. It was a bit of a struggle with the brace and my ankle, and hurt a bit. Well, quite a lot to be honest. But I was used to it.

Today was no normal Wednesday afternoon. It was my birthday, February 29th. As I'm sure you know, February usually has only 28 days, but every four years, it has an extra day. My teacher did try to explain why once, but I didn't understand. I'm not sure he did either. And eight years ago, I was born on that extra day. Which meant that I was either two or eight, I wasn't sure which. Today was my second birthday, though it was eight years since I was born. I found it all very confusing.

My Nan said that having my birthday on February 29th was good luck. That magic might happen. But Daddy said not to listen to Nan's stories, cos she was a bit, and put his finger to the side of his head and twisted it. Still, Nan was the only one who had remembered it was my birthday today. She came into my room quietly, before anyone else was awake, and gave me a present. A small glass ball, the size of a snooker ball, except you could see through it, or into it, I wasn't sure which. "To help with the magic," she said, putting a finger to her lips.

I crouched down to look at the little door more closely. It was difficult, because of the brace, and hurt, because of my ankle, but I managed. It was a perfectly normal door, except that it was the wrong size. I wondered who lived there. So, I reached out and knocked on it twice with the knocker. After a couple of seconds, the door opened and a little head poked out. The head looked this way and that until it finally noticed me crouching down in front of it. It seemed that the head was having as much trouble seeing me as I had been having seeing the door. There was a squeal of fear, and the owner of the head tried to close the door quickly, but I was even quicker and grabbed it with my hand to stop it closing.

We pulled back and forth for a few seconds until she, because the head was definitely a female head, fell backwards onto the pavement with a bump, and the door slammed shut behind her.

She was some kind of furry animal I couldn't identify. I knew I had seen others like her in one of my story books, but I couldn't remember which one. Was she an otter? No, not an otter. Maybe a badger? Or a weasel?

She was wearing a headscarf and had an apron wrapped around her waist. She quickly turned and tried to open the door, but it seemed to have locked behind her. She started banging on it frantically, but nothing happened.

"I'm sorry," I said. "I didn't mean for you to get locked out. But tell me, is there anyone else inside?"

"No," she replied.

"Then why are you banging?"

"I don't know," she said, and sat down on the ground. "Oh Dear! Oh Dear!" she cried, and started wringing her paws. She looked up at me. "They told me that no one would be able to see me. Or my door. That it was safe to live here near people because I would be invisible." She shook her head. "I don't understand it." She was almost crying. Then she looked up at me. "Do you have the magic? Is that it?"

"I don't think so," I replied.

"Then why can you see me? Unless..." She was pacing up and down now. "The exception, maybe that's it. Could today be the exception?" She paced up and down in front of her locked front door. "Now, let me remember, how did I choose the exception?"

I didn't understand what she was talking about, so decided it was best to keep quiet while she thought.

"As I'm sure you know," she glanced up at me hopefully, "with natural magic, you always have to have one exception..."

"No, I didn't know that," I replied.

"Goodness!" she said, "You humans are so funny. How on earth do you manage?" Then she looked thoughtful. Suddenly her face seemed to pale. "What is today's date?" she asked, with a fearful look.

"February 29th" I said, "It's a leap year. Today is my..."

"Oh No!" she interrupted. "Oh Dear! Oh Dear! That's it. The exception!" She stopped pacing and looked at me. "I thought I was being really clever, choosing a date that comes round only once every four years."

"That does sound like a good idea," I said.

"But the problem is, when it's only once every four years, it's so easy to forget. And that's what I did."

Like my parents with my birthday, I thought.

"Do you have a key?" I asked, trying to be helpful.

"Yes, yes, of course I have a key!" she replied sharply. Then her shoulders sagged. "It's on the kitchen table!"

"Is there another way in?" I asked. "Do you have a back door?"

"Yes, but I think it might be some way away," she replied. "Not from the inside of course, but on the outside. Space is different out here. Distances are different."

I was confused.

"How far away is Edinburgh?" she asked.

"About three hundred miles, I think. How far is the back door on the inside?"

"About twelve feet." she said.

"So what are we to do?" I asked her. I had been crouching too long and my leg was beginning to throb.

"There is only one way of getting the door to open with me on the outside," she said. "We need a spell."

"I don't know any spells, I'm afraid," I said.

She reached into her apron pocket and pulled out a tiny black book.

"Now let me see, a spell for doors...yes... here's one..."

"Do you want to try it?" I asked.

"Yes but," she shook her head," it is so difficult. We need someone, anyone, who happens...." she looked hopeless.

"Yes...who happens to what?" I asked.

"Well, to start with, it has to be someone with the magic," she said. "But also someone whose birthday it is today. How on earth are we going to find anyone like that?"

"If we can find that person?" I said, trying to keep the excitement out of my voice, "What will they have to do?"

"Nothing much," she said. "It's a really easy spell. They just have to knock on the door three times and say, *"Open for me, I don't want to stay. Open for me, it is my birthday!"*

"And if we do find this person, does anything happen to them?"

"They get a wish," she said.

"A wish?"

"Yes, whatever they want, as long as it is good. The magic doesn't work if you wish for something bad."

"So let me get this right," I said, and while I was speaking, my left hand reached into my pocket and took hold tightly of the ball Nan had given me. "If today was my birthday, and if I knocked on the door three times, like this..."

Knock Knock Knock, went my hand on the brass knocker.

"...and if I then I start saying *'Open for me, I don't want to stay...'*

"Yes, but the magic won't work unless it's your..."

'...open for me, it is my birthday.'

...actual birthday," she started to say.

At that exact moment when I said the last word of the rhyme, and we found ourselves saying the work *'birthday'* together, the little door opened. All by itself.

"Ooh!", she said, "However did you...?"

But she suddenly vanished inside, as if sucked in by a great wind. The door slammed shut behind her. Then it started to shrink, smaller and smaller, until it was hard to see, smaller and smaller until, finally, with a faint 'pop', it had vanished completely and there was nothing to say that it had ever been there.

I stood up from my crouching position. It was only after walking a few steps, and my leg no longer hurt, that I remembered my wish.

I looked down. The brace on my leg had vanished. I tried standing on my left leg. It didn't hurt. I tried hopping on my left leg. It still didn't hurt. So then I ran home as fast as any eight-year-old boy could possibly run and wondered what on earth I was going to tell my parents.

story

*The Dragon's Breath**

IT WAS A PEA-SOUPER, thick smoke sinking from the coal chimneys so dense you could almost chew it, cutting visibility to just a few inches, muffling and distorting sounds so that they seemed to come from all directions at once.

I opened the blue door, at least I assumed it was still blue, and paused, listening carefully. Eventually I heard them. The footsteps that had been following me through the London fog for the last half hour. Still there. Herman. That's what I called him. My follower. My assassin. Herman.

Having an eidetic memory can have its disadvantages. Especially when what you remember is vital intelligence about a new rocket the Nazis were developing. I knew Herman had to show up eventually. And now, in November 1943, he was here.

On a night like this, what with the blackout and the fog creating swirling shapes which appear and disappear, it would be so easy to believe in the supernatural. Hidden doors leading to strange worlds containing who-knows-what devilish creatures. I smiled to myself. I belonged on a night like this. I was in my element.

I realised that Herman might be having trouble keeping up, so after unlocking the door I paused for a moment or two, just to make sure he didn't lose me. Then I entered, closing but not locking, the blue door behind me, and walked quickly straight ahead. Everything was pitch black, of course, but that didn't slow me down. I concentrated, remembering and picturing my surroundings from earlier visits. I reached out my hand and there it was, the cracked wall, just as I remembered. I turned and descended the stairs, counting carefully. One hundred and twenty-three steps. At every step the air seemed to get more stale. And warmer.

It is surprising, when in total darkness, how quickly other senses develop to compensate. My hearing and my smell and even my sense of touch all seemed enhanced. I could smell the rats and hear them scurrying out of my way. And I could sense small changes in the air on my face. And yes, it was definitely getting hotter.

Half way down I paused. And listened beyond the rustling rats to the noises filtering down from above. I heard the blue door opening and closing, the quiet cursing and the lighting of a match. For light rather than a cigarette, I decided. Or maybe both.

Suddenly I detected a slight shifting in the air and a groaning in the distance. As if a subterranean dragon had woken from hibernation too early and was angry. The noise increased rapidly to a roar and a wave of putrid air swept by me. And then, of course, I thought of Alice and Jimmy. Poor Jimmy. I shook my head. No time to remember them now. I had to stay alert. As quickly as it had come, the roar diminished and the air became still once more.

I continued down the steps until I reached the bottom. It was hot down here, and the air was rank. As if I had ventured into the dragon's lair. I knew that I was now standing in a small area where the passageway opened out into a long narrow chamber. I could see it clearly in my mind's eye. Every detail. I entered, turned left, walked three steps, and waited with my back to the wall. I had just four minutes until the next time it came. The dragon's breath. Four minutes.

I listened carefully. The footsteps following me were cautious and hesitant, punctuated frequently by the sound of swearing as match burnt down to finger, and then the scraping sound of a fresh Swan Vesta being struck on the wall. At one point I heard a loud grunt and a thud, as if something had been kicked against a wall. "Fucking rats!" I heard. The accent was Irish.

Herman was getting close now. I could hear every footstep as he crunched through broken glass, and even caught the smell of cheap after-shave mixed with stale B.O. wafting past me as he entered the chamber. I smelt too his fear and uncertainty. I smiled. He had no idea what kind of subterranean world he had ventured into. No idea what was waiting for him. He didn't know about the dragon's breath. He had no idea where he was.

I held my breath. I judged he was four feet ahead and to the right of me.

Then there was that movement of the air again, and the roaring noise of something approaching at great speed. I heard him curse as the wind blew out his match. For an instant he too was in total darkness. He gasped in fear.

It had to be now! I ran forward and shoulder-charged him. Caught him right in the middle of his back. I heard his cry of shock and surprise, and then the sound of him falling over the edge into the void below. And then it was upon us like an angry monster, rumbling and screeching and roaring and battering us with its foul-smelling breath.

Then it was gone. And Herman too was gone.

I made my way back up the one hundred and twenty-three steps to the blue door, locking it carefully behind me with my key. I had known it would come in handy one day, that key.

I had worked here once, you see. Down Street, one of London's lost Underground stations, had closed in 1932. On the Piccadilly line. Trains every four minutes. None stopped nowadays of course.

Churchill's War cabinet relocated here for a few months in 1940, while the War Rooms were being built under Whitehall. I was assigned here then as MI5 liaison.

I had only worked here for a short while, though, when the blitz came, and the bomb which took away Alice and Jimmy, and my home, and my colours and, well, just about everything except my memory.

It was little Jimmy who called it 'the Dragon's Breath' when he was four – the wind that preceded a train along the tunnel as it pulled into a station.

Time to make my way back to Whitehall to make my report. Someone would have to be on hand, at the next station, or maybe the end of the line, to clean Herman's remains from the front of the train.

I turned and walked towards Hyde Park Corner, whistling quietly to myself, visualizing the pavement ahead, rattling my white cane on the railings as I went.

*The Dream**

At first he ignored it
But it kept recurring
Not vague and insubstantial and quick to fade
As dreams usually are
But vivid and insistent
Always exactly the same

He was walking into the forest with his axe
And chopping down a tree
From the copse of cypress
At the bottom of the mountain
Then dragging the log back home
The clincher was a smiling face and soft voice
That reminded him of his mother
A warm feeling of security
Like being held in her arms
So he thought "What the hell?"

The first couple of trees he managed alone
Then one morning he found his eldest son
Walking axe in hand beside him
Soon the whole family was helping
They never discussed why
Or what the wood might be for
He suspected they were having dreams
Of their own

* * *

Then one night the dream changed
He saw a huge boat
Resting in the field near their house
Far too big for his small family
And far too big for the small creek

That snaked through their farm
They were twenty miles from the sea after all

The following morning one of his sons
Brought him some detailed plans
For a boat over 400ft long and 70ft wide
He didn't ask where the plans had come from

They started building
The neighbours thought he was crazy
People came from miles around
To see
To laugh at him
It was hard work too
The hottest summer anyone could remember
The soil parched and cracked
His shoulders blistering in the sun

Finally the boat was ready
"There's enough room for fifty in that" they said
"And there's only the five of them"

* * *

Then his dreams changed again
His mother
For he was sure now it was she
Led him to the grassland behind their hut
Where a couple of deer were grazing
She smiled and pointed
He went there the following morning
And found the deer
He thought he might have a hard job
Chasing and catching them
But they seemed happy to follow him home
Maybe they too were having dreams

That night in his dream
She led him to a different place

Death and Birth and In Between

This time in the forest
Where two wild boar were rooting under a tree
Yet again when he went to the place
The following morning
He found the boar
And yet again they followed him home
Like obedient children

Then foxes and wolves
And all manner of other creatures
Some familiar
Some he'd never seen before
Some walking on the ground
Some slithering through the grasses
Some flying in the air
He had to extend his yard twice
To accommodate them all

Strangely
Together in the same yard
Predator and prey
Nothing ate the other
All the creatures remained there peacefully
As if waiting for something

* * *

Then came the final dream
He loaded the boat with their entire food store
Everything they had put aside for the winter
As well as anything else
They could buy from neighbours

The following morning he led the animals
Carefully up a gangplank into the boat
Then the whole family joined him
And they raised the plank

Death and Birth and In Between

For three days they sat there
Feeling quite ridiculous to be honest
Five people and scores of animals
Together in a boat
In a field on dry land
At one point there were over fifty people
Standing round pointing and laughing

It was then
for the first and only time
That his wife questioned him
"Are you sure about this Noah?"
He simply smiled and nodded
Thinking about his mother

On the fourth afternoon the weather changed
The scorching sunshine was replaced
By dark clouds and a fierce wind

Then the rain came

story

The End of the World

OVER THE CENTURIES God has just lost interest in us. In the early years, he was interfering all the time, sending down plagues of frogs, and parting the sea so his favourite tribe could escape from their enemies, or sending (some say) his son to set an example, or when that didn't work sending (others say) an emissary to dictate an entire book to an illiterate shepherd in a cave, just to help us get things right. But we never listened, never let him get the last word, and so he just lost interest and occupied himself elsewhere and let us get on with it.

He is very busy, you know, and has several really interesting projects on the go at any one time.

So when the world was on the brink, and the wild animals were all gone, and nothing swam in the sea except jellyfish, and nothing flew in the air except mosquitos, and nothing grew in the ground except nettles, and nothing crawled on the land except cockroaches and rats, he glanced back in our direction, snorted at the mess we'd made of it all, clicked his fingers with a snap, yawned, and the world as we knew it ended.

Everyone vanished in that instant. And God looked down, and saw that it was good, or at least better, smiled and turned his attentions back elsewhere.

But in his haste, he had overlooked one young man, living in a tent in the desert. This man was left alone in the world with all that devastation, the barren earth beneath his feet, and the barren sea around it, and the barren sky above. While God was preoccupied, this man wandered through all this desolation.

Eventually he found one small corner of this waste land with one tiny garden ravaged less by the devastation, with a few roots and leaves and fruit growing. And this young man dug some roots, and picked some leaves, and ate some fruit, and learned how to cultivate the soil, to banish the nettles and rats. Soon a few surviving bees (they hadn't all died after all) found their way to his garden, and buzzed from plant to plant, and there were fish swimming again in the stream (neither had they), and the sound of birdsong could be heard once more (nor them).

But this man was alone, and he was lonely, so he invented a god to pray to. He asked for a companion, someone with whom to share his garden. And his prayer was heard, though not by the god he invented, and one evening, while this man slept, let us call him Adam, God took a superfluous rib from his side and fashioned a companion for him, let us call her Eve. And they lived together in this garden, let us call it Eden, quite happily for a very long time.

Until one morning they started arguing, about whether or not they should eat an apple from one particular tree. And God glanced back and sighed, and muttered "Here we go again" under his breath and with a shake of his head decided to turn his attentions to one of his other more rewarding projects for a while.

Mankind was such hard work.

*Flotsam**

IT IS THE SUPERMARKET TROLLEY he sees first, as it noses its way cautiously through the doors, and his heart sinks. Three days running now. It can't go on. PC Fox shakes his head and speaks into his phone, all the time his eyes following her shuffling progress across the concourse.

She is old, but how old is difficult to guess. Her hair hangs like tangled seaweed onto her shoulders, failing to hide the encrusted grime at the back of her neck. She must have had teeth once, maybe even pride, but today she has neither. Following the trolley across the station concourse, she seems to carry her own space with her. The flood of commuters divides and flows round her, an ancient rock in their turbulent river.

His call finished, he continues watching. She shows no sign of leaving. The trolley has led her to the middle of the concourse, and there she stops. She stands, in her bubble of empty space, next to the television screens showing train arrivals, although she gives no sign that she can read or even see them. She is wearing what might once have been a yellow coat, or is it a dressing gown, above a pair of bright green Wellington boots. For a long while she waits, her dull eyes unfocussed.

Eventually he takes an uncertain step towards her, but then stops. They'll be coming for her soon. They said within half an hour. It can't be long now. Maybe best just to wait.

A few minutes later the London train arrives, discharging its cargo of passengers like water through a sluice. The station quickly empties again. Or at least nearly empties. Once the flood of commuters has departed, a young man remains standing, looking around. He too seems out of place, part of the flotsam of society washed up on the shore of this unfamiliar station.

PC Fox studies him warily. His hair is knotted into dreadlocks, dyed green on one side. He is wearing three bars through one eyebrow and two rings through the opposite nostril. He has a snake tattoo encircling one forearm.

Thoughts flood though PC Fox's mind: Christ, what have we got here? Wonder what's in the bag. Odds on I'll get a drugs bust if I take him in, I can almost smell the stuff just looking at him. He's not that big. Can I handle him on my own? Maybe I ought to ring for backup? But the women PCs will be here any minute to deal with the old girl. Maybe best to just wait and watch.

The young man sees the old woman and stares at her for long time. Then he slowly approaches.

PC Fox is alert. It's the wrong time of day for a mugging, but you can never be sure. Mind you, it's unlikely that the old girl has anything worth nicking.

The young man gently takes her hand and strokes it, looking into her eyes.

"I came as soon as I heard," he says.

She raises her eyes when she hears his voice, and they slowly focus on his face and for the first time become alive.

"Look at the state of you, Nan. How long has it been this time? Come on, I'll take you back. We'll soon get you sorted."

The young man picks her carrier bags from the trolley and, carrying them easily in one hand, he leads her out of the concourse. In a few moments they have vanished through the doors.

Only the empty supermarket trolley remains where she had been standing.

story

Fog

"**I THINK WE'RE LOST!**" Dad said, leaning forward over the steering wheel and peering into the fog. It was hard to see anything at all – the headlights were worse than useless, their light bouncing back from the white wall into our eyes rather than piercing it.

"It seems to be getting thicker," said Mum smugly. She had argued against going to visit Aunt Marge in this weather and, being extremely superstitious, felt that venturing out at Halloween at all was in itself risky.

"Can you all keep your eyes peeled for any road sign?" Dad asked. "Sedgeford can't be too far away now." He had decided to cut across country on an unmarked back road that pointed vaguely in the right direction.

"Strange that you never noticed that road before," said Mum. There was a slight tremor in her voice. "What was the last village called?"

"Old Marsh Rising, I think," said Dad.

"I can't find it on the map," I said, trying to be helpful. My brother Malcolm kicked me. Just then we passed a village sign on our left.

"What did it say? What did it say?" Mum asked.

"Oh, something End, Wood End, maybe. Began with a 'W'."

"Could it have been Witch End?" Malcolm asked innocently, trying not to be too obvious about looking at Mum's expression from the corner of his eye.

We drove slowly into the village. The fog was thinner here. We passed a white thatched cottage on our left, and a dilapidated barn on our right, and then a traditional village green with a duckpond next to a crossroads. There was a signpost, an old-fashioned type with black writing on white fingers. There were fingers pointing ahead, left and right. The finger pointing back down the road we had come from was missing. Dad got out and peered up at the signpost. I saw him take off his glasses, wipe them on his handkerchief, put them back on his nose, and peer up again. He returned to the car shaking his head.

"Can't make it out," he said. "Never mind. We can ask at the pub." He drove straight over the crossroads. But there was no pub. In fact, there was no sign of life at all. Not even the ubiquitous old man walking his dog. And suddenly we were through the village and into the dense fog again. We drove on for a few minutes, and then passed another village sign.

"This village is also called 'Something-beginning-with-W End, "Dad said, chuckling. "Norfolk…typical!" Just then we drove past a white thatched cottage on our left and a dilapidated barn on our right.

"Weird," Dad said. "Looks just like the last place."

Actually, I thought it looked identical to the last place, and wasn't at all surprised when we came to an identical cross roads beside an identical village green with an identical duckpond.

"You could try asking the ducks for directions," said Malcolm. We ignored him.

"Doesn't this look just like the last village?" Mum croaked. I could see in the driving mirror that her face was now white.

"Not quite," I said. "The road sign is different, look!" We all looked. On this sign there were fingers pointing left and right, but not ahead or behind.

"Bloody vandals," said Dad.

"Language! Children!" said Mum. Dad ignored her.

"I'll try this way, he said, turning left. The road quickly exited the village, back into the fog, which was now thicker than ever. Then after a few miles we yet again passed the now familiar white thatched cottage and dilapidated barn and came to the crossroads beside the duckpond.

We sat in silence. No one commented on the fact that everything was again exactly the same. We all looked at the road sign in silence. There was only the one finger now, pointing right. Dad turned right.

Death and Birth and In Between

I don't think any of us was surprised when we found ourselves coming back into the village again. We all knew that it was the same village, however impossible that seemed.

This time there was no road sign at the crossroads, just a decaying post which might have once displayed fingers, but was now only adorned with moss.

"Look!" said Malcolm, pointing. There was an elderly man, with a bird's nest beard and a beret, throwing fragments of bread to the ducks. Dad got out of the car. I got out too. Mum and Malcolm stayed put. We walked over. The man looked startled to see us.

"I wonder if you can help us," Dad said. "We seem to be lost."

"Yes, yes…we don't get many visitors here nowadays," the old man said. He looked confused. "In fact I can't remember the last time." Then a thought seemed to strike him. "What date is it today?" he asked.

"October 31st." Dad said, and waved his arm towards a candlelit pumpkin in a nearby window. "Halloween."

"Ah, that explains it," the old man said. He then glanced towards the road sign. "You've been here a while I see." We both turned and looked at the sign, wondering what he meant. But when we turned back, he had vanished.

"How rude!" Dad said, "I didn't even have a chance to ask him how to get to Sedgeford."

Just then Malcolm came running up. "There's a noticeboard over here, by the church hall" he said. "You've got to come and look."

We walked over. There was just one notice.

"Welcome to our village," it said. "You are now at Witts End."

song

Follow Me! *

I wrote a poem once about a place in Spain,
I went back there recently, it was not the same.
I wrote a song once about a girl I knew,
Told her that I loved her, maybe that was not true.
I tried to write a book while living on a farm,
Didn't do any good though, don't think it did any harm.
I've got a fantasy about living in a commune with some friends,
Don't know if it'll materialise, 'spose I'll find out in the end.

    And I have travelled on the slightest whim or inclination,
    And I have floated on the breeze,
    And I have loved, I must admit sometimes unwisely,
    And I have managed to stay free.

And so I'm telling you my life has been just fine,
Done nothing I'm ashamed of, made the most of time,
Had my share of fantasies, I've had my hopes and fears,
Laughed my share of laughter, cried my share of tears.
But now I'm stuck just like a lion in your net,
Like a cockroach in the treacle, like a fly within your web.
It wasn't what I wanted. It wasn't what I planned.
But now I feel this way please take my reaching hand.

    You see, I'm missing you
    Much more than I ever thought I would,
    I think about you every day.
    And so I'm asking you to come on an adventure,
    As this request I'm going to make.

        Come on and follow me into the sun,
        My island's much too big for one,
        I know that you and I can love and have fun here.
        We'll go swimming on Xmas day,
        Watch flying fish skimming over the waves,
        And in the evening sing our songs of happy days.
        Come on and take my reaching hand,
        Grenada, this'll be our promised land,

Death and Birth and In Between

And we will write our names in love in the sand.
Come on and follow me. Put your trust in me.
Together we'll be free, here in Grenada.

And I don't know why I start to cry
And die inside when I call out your name.
I wake in the night, sweating with fright,
Wondering if I will ever see you again.

So, I remember the days
In the south of France and in Spain,
A double bed in a broke-down shed
And we couldn't see the mountains for rain.
A forest in Sweden one night,
Man, how those mosquitos could bite.
A funny photograph in Tivoli then after
We played around for a while.
Do you remember? Do you remember?
Santa Christina! Santa Christina!

Santa Christina's a magical place
And we worshipped there for a couple of days
Praying our prayers to the Goddess of the Sea.
We slept our nights away on the beach,
And for breakfast we had one peach each,
And then we made love, my Finnish girl and me.

> I love that girl.
> I miss that girl.
> Have I lost that girl?

We took off our clothes to be free.
I touched her and she touched me.
Then I took her hand, we skipped over the sand and then
Splashed naked into the sea.

> Was it you who said, "We'll know
> How much we love when you go"?
> Was it me who said, "That's fine,
> See how we feel in two years' time"?

Death and Birth and In Between

Was it you who wet my hair
With tears the last time we were together there?
Now it's me who wants to cry.
Will you let me change my mind?

We travelled together last summer so far,
A couple of packs and a battered guitar,
All the way from Scandinavia to the Mediterranean.
Standing beside those roads with no doubt,
Smiles on our faces, our thumbs sticking out,
We floated our way wherever the breeze would take us.
We lived for the present, we lived for our hearts
Squeezed into the back of a hundred small cars,
Till we washed up on a beach in the Costa Brava.
Travelling with you felt so right.
We hitch-hiked in the day, slept rough at night.
And then you went back to school, and I flew to Grenada.

If you were a boy, you'd have to join the army for a year,
But you're not you're a girl and so you're free for a year,
So get on a plane and join me here.
I'll find a flat with a view fit for a king,
Treat you like a princess, write songs we can sing,
And if our love works out, I'll buy you a ring.

    And we will travel on the slightest whim or inclination,
    And we will float upon the breeze,
    And we will love, I truly hope not too unwisely,
    And here together we'll be free.

        Come on and follow me into the Sun,
        My island's much too big for one,
        I know that you and I can love and have fun here.
        We'll go swimming on Xmas day,
        Watch flying fish skimming over the waves,
        And in the evening sing our songs of happy days.
        Come on and take my reaching hand,
        Grenada, this'll be our promised land,
        And we will write our names in love in the sand.
        Come on and follow me. Put your trust in me.
        Together we'll be free, here in Grenada.

*Fool's Gold**

Looking for redemption,
Fearing for my soul,
The route to true salvation
Buried like the Dead Sea scrolls.
Did he walk on water?
Did he really raise the dead?
How could he feed five thousand
With only fish and bread?

> *Tell me did they really happen*
> *All these stories we've been told?*
> *Or was he just a charlatan,*
> *Peddling nuggets of fool's gold*?

Did he come from elsewhere?
Was he human or divine?
Did he uproot the tree in Eden?
Was he angelic or serpentine?
Some say he was an alien
With his own ecstatic dream,
Or maybe just some sick delusional
With a power-hungry scheme.

Should I decide to follow
For the comfort I might feel,
Even if belief is hollow,
Just like spinning a prayer wheel?
Surely they can't all be wrong.
I'm totally confused.
But I don't want to be an atheist
With no belief to lose.

Tell me did they really happen
All these stories we've been told?
Or was he just a charlatan,
Peddling nuggets of fool's gold?

Hoping for redemption,
Praying for relief,
The route to true salvation
Simply beggars all belief.
I am a man of science,
Trained to require proof,
Blind faith is not an option,
Belief not shatterproof.

Prove to me they really happened
All these stories we've been told.
Prove he wasn't just a charlatan
Peddling nuggets of fool's gold.

This road is never ending,
This fog will never rise,
I take one step after another
Stumbling over buried lies.
I don't know where I'm going,
And I can't say where I've been.
Is all this blind meandering
Part of some celestial scheme?

Maybe Buddha has the answer,
Or the Gods of the Hindus,
Or maybe it's Mohammad,
Or Yahweh of the Jews.
The thing is they can't all be right,
I'm totally confused.
I close my eyes to pray but I
Don't know which God to choose.

Did Jesus really rise up from the
Dead so we'd be saved?
Did Mohammad really meet
Archangel Gabriel in that cave?
Did Moses really raise his staff
And separate the sea?
Did Buddha really find enlightenment
Under that tree?

> *Tell me did they really happen*
> *All the stories we've been told?*
> *Or were they all just charlatans*
> *Peddling nuggets of fool's gold?*
>
> *Were they all just charlatans*
> *These holy men of old?*
> *Or was one of them the real deal,*
> *Offering a nugget of pure gold?*

song

*For Us**

Walking down the beach one day
I looked into her eyes
Saw a tear appearing there
It came as some surprise
Didn't know I'd hurt her
Didn't know I could
Didn't understand just where I stood

Kissed the tear away
It was salty on my tongue
Kissed each of her eyelids
And her smile shone through like sun
Maybe it was madness
Or maybe the blue sky
Or maybe it was love that made us high

I'd like to know
How did it show?
Without the use of words
I felt the message flow
I'd like to see,
Just what might be
Find out what life might have in store
For you and me

The sun will shine for us
Weather stay fine for us
Grapes turn to wine for us
We'll drink our fill

Death and Birth and In Between

Song birds will wake for us
The waves will break for us
The earth will quake for us
And clocks stand still

Angels will sing for us
Church bells will ring for us
Life is waiting for us
We're on our way

The extra mile for us
The moon will smile on us
Mermaids will cry for us
Turn night to day

Blossom will fall for us
Daughters grow tall for us
Break down the wall for us
And clamber through

Rivers will flow for us
Oracles know for us
Grandchildren grow for us
For me and you
For me and you

poem

Fox Hunting

in the early hours
she visits
as most nights
knowing eventually
inevitably
I will slip up

a tiny mistake
a new bed
soil turned over
too close to the run
soft earth an invitation
to dig

now six heads and six bodies
lay scattered amongst
the feathers and the leaves
nothing eaten
nothing taken

killing for fun

Gethsemane Again

We broke our bread
And sipped our wine
And you yielded to my forty
Phrases of silver-tongued deceit
As I knew you would

But afterwards
As the moonlight painted a cross
On the Golgotha of your bed
Transfixing you where you lay
Bathing your lost innocence
In a milky glow
Your eyes reached
And pleaded
And accused
There on the bloodied altar-sheet
Of our passion
For words I was three times
Unable to utter

I kissed your cheek
But you turned your head away
And flinched
As if it were Gethsemane again
And my lips were thorns

In the silence that followed
The halo of smoke from your cigarette
Reached through the still air in judgement
And nestled round my neck
Like a noose

Death and Birth and In Between

I stumbled from the room
Lit by the red flickering glow from your lava lamp
Watched jealously by posters of boybands
Your judgement tolling in my ear

And ran to the taxi waiting like a Judas tree
In the street outside
Wondering all the time
Why it was me
That was crying

Death and Birth and In Between

story

The Girl on Blades

HE IS IN UNIFORM. The black uniform with gold braid on his shoulders and a crest on his breast pocket. There's the peaked cap that goes with it too. It makes him feel, well, taller, somehow, and the thin grey military moustache adds to the image.

As he walks through the Mall, with a confident stride, he has an air of authority. He is waiting. Waiting for something, he's not exactly sure what, to happen.

It is the last Saturday before Christmas, and the Mall is heaving with shoppers, but somehow the girl on rollerblades manages to sail through them as if they don't exist. iPod belted to her waist, headphones glued to her ears, she barely seems to notice the throng as she skims past. A jink here, a curve there, always missing, never colliding.

The man purses his lips when he sees her. He recognises her immediately. Those red lips, held in a fixed pout. The hair, streaming behind in an unsecured fan. He is doubtful for a moment, uncertain. He's not exactly sure what she's up to, but he watches carefully.

And then it happens. A middle-aged woman steps out of Boots and instead of dipping past the girl slams into her. A cry. Bags flying through the air. Then the girl is all apologies, kneeling on the floor, picking up the scattered packages, helping stuff them back into the carrier bags, stammering her words.

He hurries over to them both. "You should be more careful, young lady. Skating is not allowed in here. And now you can see why."

"I'm so sorry, it was…I didn't…"

But he is ignoring her now.

"Are you alright madam? Are you injured at all?"

He is reaching down and helping the woman back onto her feet.

"No…no…I think I'm alright. Thank you." The smile she gives him is in stark contrast to the icy glare the girl receives.

"I am so terribly sorry…"

"Be off with you!!" he says fiercely.

"But…."

"Be gone! You're finished here."

She needs no further encouragement and within seconds she is gone, through the swing doors, out on to the street, and away. Meanwhile he is brushing down the woman's coat and handing her the last of her bags.

"Now are you sure you're alright?"

"Yes fine…"

A look of consternation flashes across her face. She quickly rummages in her handbag, and then looks around her feet.

"My purse!! It's gone. She stole my purse!!"

"Are you sure?"

"Yes, it was in this bag here. She must have taken it as she was picking up the shopping. Ohhhhh!"

"Was there much in it?"

"Yes!" Now she is crying. "All my Christmas money. About six hundred pounds."

"What did it look like?"

"Brown leather, with wooden beads along the top. It was a present from my granddaughter."

He shakes his head in sympathy. "She's well away now, I'm afraid."

He glances up at the doors, then he leads her to a bench.

"You sit down here. I'll phone for the police. Don't you worry. They'll catch her. We know what she looks like."

Then he too has left her, striding out of one of the side doors, a new sense of purpose in his step. He walks up the steps, through another swing door, hesitates just for a moment in front of a door bearing the message "Staff Only" before moving quickly along the corridor to the car park.

* * *

Two minutes later and he is in his car, driving down the hill towards the river. He pulls up outside the cinema and throws open the door.

"Get in!!" he says.

She hesitates for a second.

"Quickly, I can't wait all day."

She jumps into the car and they are away. The rollerblades are gone now, the hair stuffed up inside a beret. But the lips are the same, deep red and pouting. As they cross the bridge, he takes off his hat and throws it into the back.

"How did you do today?" he asks.

"Fine. Two purses, three wallets, a pearl necklace and a couple of nice watches. I missed the old girl at the end though. Too many people around."

He laughs and takes something from his hip pocket. It is a brown leather purse, with wooden beads along the top.

"It's alright, I finished that one off for you."

She smiles, leans over, unpeels his fake moustache before kissing him on the cheek.

"You're the best, you are, you know that? So, where shall we go tomorrow, Granddad?"

story

Going Home

I AM SITTING ON THE TRAIN on my way home from work. I have made this trip hundreds of times and know every inch of the route. Often the train is so crowded I have to stand, but today it is surprisingly empty and I have a compartment to myself. I settle down and start to read. It is the latest Dick Francis novel. I like his books. All about horse-racing. Hopefully I will be able to finish the chapter before we reach Streatham Common Station. From there it is just a short walk home.

After a while I hear a noise and glance up. I am surprised to find that that there is a woman sitting opposite. I don't remember her getting on. Sometimes when I'm reading, I get so engrossed that I don't notice what's happening around me. I return to my novel but find myself reading the same paragraph over and over again. There is something about the lady that disturbs me. She looks familiar somehow. I glance up again. She is smiling at me.

This is embarrassing. I shuffle nervously in my seat.

"Hello, Dad," she says.

I look away. You do get some strange people on trains nowadays.

"I think you are mistaken young lady."

"You must stop doing this," she says.

I am uncomfortable and want to ignore her. But I can't.

"Doing what?" I ask.

"Wandering off. You know it makes them upset. They nearly called the police this time."

"I think you're mistaken, young lady." I tell her again. "And stop calling me 'Dad'. You know full well I'm not your father."

Her smile vanishes and she looks away.

"I only have one child," I say, "my daughter Jenny. She is seven."

She looks at me sadly, and pauses before replying. "I am your daughter," she says, "and my name is Jenny, but I'm thirty-five now."

She is starting to scare me. I look around but there is no one else in the compartment who can help.

"Where are you going?" she asks.

"I'm going home."

"Where's that?"

I open my mouth to speak, but then stop. Why can't I remember? That happens sometimes. Things I know so well slip away and hide for a while. I close my eyes and concentrate. Then it comes to me.

"Abercairn Road," I say. "It's in Streatham."

She smiles sadly. "You used to live there. We all did. That's where I grew up. But you moved away from Streatham when Mum died. You live at Greenacres nowadays."

"What's Greenacres?"

"It's a care home," she said. "It's where you live. You like it there."

I look at her for a long while. There is something about what she is saying that strikes a chord. Like grasping for a dream when you wake up.

Then she hands me a raincoat. "Put this on. You can't wander round like that."

I look down and realise I am wearing only pyjamas. Is this a dream? It feels like a dream. That's what happens in dreams, isn't it? You find yourself in the wrong place in your pyjamas. I take the coat obediently and put it on. She reaches over and gently takes the book from me. She looks at the cover.

"Still reading the same book, I see."

"It's the latest Dick Francis," I say. "I like his books. All about horse racing."

The train starts to slow. She puts the book in her bag. "We get off at the next station," she says. "Gareth is waiting there with the car. He'll drive us back."

"Who's Gareth?"

"My husband."

Then she reaches into her bag and offers me a tissue. "Use this," she says.

I don't understand what she means.

"Never mind. Let me."

She reaches over and wipes away the tears that are inexplicably running down my cheeks.

*Golden Slippers**

"THESE ARE BEAUTIFUL," I said, reaching out to them. They were a pair of tiny golden slippers, small – maybe little girl's slippers – but beautiful, with a deep, glowing colour.

"Please...do not...touch."

The words came in short bursts, punctuated by painful wheezes.

"They are old now, and fragile. But very valuable. The fabric – it is made from woven gold."

Several seconds more wheezing.

"They are mine. I used to wear them. When I was much younger, you will understand."

Sal had a tube up his left nostril and a drip connected to his left arm. But as always, I was struck by the face. A patchwork of deep crevices stretched over ancient black parchment, with a toothless gummy mouth that seemed all lips and spit. Yet underneath the ravages of age, I could see that it had once been a beautiful face.

It is always difficult, when people are dying, to know how much of what they tell you is the truth, and how much their imagination. Sal was starting to breathe easier now, as the morphine took effect. He turned to me, and I was struck again at the beauty in those ancient dark eyes, still clear, and the intelligence behind them.

"Tell me about them," I said.

Sal paused for a long while.

"They told me I was a beautiful child," he said. "Not my parents, I don't really remember them. But the others in the palace. It was what they used to say. And later the Prince too." Sal turned and coughed. There was more blood than last time, I noticed, red and frothy. I cleaned his mouth and he continued.

"I don't remember much before the palace. My parents sold me when I was very young, you see. I remember there was a long, long, journey across desert. There were other children like me, black and young, sold to the blue men. It was normal. Beautiful children were a commodity like any other – goats, camels. You had any to spare, you sold them. It was all the same in those days. A beautiful child could fetch a lot of money.

"I can clearly remember the market in Marrakech. There was an auction. I was on a platform, like a stage, with several other children. The heat of the sun, and the strange smell of spices everywhere. The people crowding round, feeling my legs, my chest, looking at my teeth, even touching my crotch. They could do what they liked. The bidding went high, very high for me, I was told. But the Prince would not be beaten. And that was how I came to live in the palace.

"I must have been about seven when I first went there. I don't know, exactly, there was no one to tell me. I always start from my years with the Prince, then count backwards. I lived with the women, in the harem. They made a big fuss of me. I was the only child there. That was strange, of course. You would expect a harem to be full of children, but the Prince…I don't know, he was…how do you say…?" One more wrinkle creased his forehead, "Oh yes…firing blanks, I suppose.

"Most nights Mahmoud waddled in with the golden slippers, the ones over there on the shelf. Yes, the very same slippers. Mahmoud came in and presented them to one of the girls. He was our guard, but also he cared for us. He was the only man we ever saw apart from the Prince. He was a eunuch, of course. There would then be a great fuss, and all of the others would gather round and make the chosen girl beautiful for the Prince. Some were jealous, of course, the girls that the Prince had not chosen, some were relieved, but still they all did their best for each other. When she left to go to him, they all sang a special song for her. It was wonderful."

Sal's eyes closed for a few seconds. I heard the gentle humming of a tune. "Sometimes the girl would come back early, sometimes not until the morning. You could never tell. Sometimes she would return in tears, sometimes with laughter. And sometimes she would hold her feelings inside. You had to watch carefully, then, for the signs to see how it had gone – the secret smile, or the escaping tear, small signs we watched for." Sal paused for a while, a long while. His eyes were closed. I could see he was struggling.

There is always a fine line you have to tread. Too much morphine would kill him, but not enough and he would feel the pain. I went over to him. I didn't think he was hurting. It seemed to be something else. Maybe simply a struggle with emotions and memories.

And I wondered then, as I have wondered many times since, how much of what Sal told me was true memory, and how much flavoured by time, imagination and morphine.

Eventually he opened his eyes and continued. "The Prince didn't call for me at first – I was too small. I was an investment for the future, they said. But I knew eventually that it would be my turn. That was why I was there, with the women in the harem.

"Then one evening, after living several years at the palace, it happened. The slippers came for me. The women had told me what to expect. I knew why I was there, knew why the Prince had bought me. But still I was scared.

"They fussed around as usual, put charcoal on my eyes, and drops from a cactus to make my pupils large. They rubbed the juice from a special berry to make my lips red, and bathed me carefully. Then they brushed my hair, which was long and thick and came to my waist. They dressed me in silks, put the golden slippers on my feet. And then they sang the song for me. It was a wonderful moment, my special time. Then Mahmoud led me to the Prince's chambers."

Sal looked at me with those ancient, beautiful eyes. "It is difficult to believe now, of course, when you see me, but I was beautiful once. And that evening – my first evening with the Prince – he made me feel that I was the most beautiful of them all." Sal vanished into the world of memory again, into his morphine dream world.

I waited. I had nowhere else to be. Sal had paid the agency top fees and more to be nursed through his last days at home, and my shift wouldn't end till six am. I looked at my watch, and then at the failing body on the bed in front of me. Eleven-thirty. Somehow, I didn't think he would last till morning. I knew the signs, had seen them too many times. Sal was almost there. Just when I thought I would never hear the end of his story, those beautiful dark eyes opened again, and Sal continued.

"The Prince was very kind. He was gentle with me. I was still a virgin the following morning, when I returned to the harem. I didn't tell the others of course. Mahmoud brought the slippers to me again the following evening, and then the Prince did take me, but he was gentle, very gentle, so that I wouldn't feel any pain. After that, I was one of his favourites. Mahmoud brought the slippers to me at least once a week.

"The last time I was with him, he looked at me, at the changes happening to my voice, my body, at the hair starting to appear at my crotch, and said, 'It will not be long now. Then we will have to decide what to do with you.'

Sal paused again, recovering memories that I could see were difficult.

"That night was our last. We made love many times. But in the morning, when I awoke, the Prince was still and cold in the bed next to me. They said afterwards it was his heart. I was devastated.

"The girls and I stayed in the palace for a further few months. It was interesting to wander the corridors and halls freely, we had never done that before. But at night we returned to the harem, and Mahmoud guarded us. I'm not sure why, or from whom, but we felt safer sleeping together, as we had always done, with him at the door.

"But soon the French came, and everything changed. If the Prince had still been alive, it would have been different. But he was dead. So they took us all away. I worked in Tangier for a while, then managed to come to London during the war.

"What work did you do?" I asked.

Sal smiled at me. "What could I do? I did the only thing I had been trained for. I..." But harsh coughing interrupted him, and this time the pillow was filled with thick red blood. I cleaned up, changed the pillowcase, and when everything was clean and calm, we settled down again.

"They let me keep the slippers. There was no one after me. I was the last. So the slippers were still mine."

His eyes closed and I could see that things were starting to get

Death and Birth and In Between

more painful again.

"And there were also his jewels. I knew where the Prince kept them. And before I left his chambers and told anyone that he had died, I took a few of the smaller ones and hid them, you know, inside me. I swallowed them."

Another bout of uncontrolled coughing interrupted him.

"I think it is time for more morphine, nurse," he said. As I stood up, the hand reached over and, rested on my arm.

"I want enough morphine this time." His beautiful, intelligent eyes pleaded with me. "You understand?"

I understood. He was paying top whack to be nursed at home, away from the inquisitive eyes of other nurses and doctors.

"This should be enough," I said, as I withdrew the needle. "You shouldn't feel any more pain now."

Sal only spoke once more. It was very laboured, and towards the end his voice became fainter. It was hard to understand everything.

"You are the only one I have ever told, in all these years…the first. You have been kind…I want you to do something for me." He smiled. "Something else…I want you to take the slippers…Put them in your bag now, so you don't forget…Then you will always remember my story…And the slippers will tell you it was true…How a young black boy became a Prince's lover."

His eyes closed, but the mouth was still moving, almost soundlessly, as the morphine carried him away. I leant over and put my ear next to his mouth, but I couldn't make out what he was saying. Then it was over.

I made a telephone call. The doctor quickly came and signed the relevant papers. He had only one question for me.

"What time did Mr …um…Abdulaziz pass away, Miss Johnson?"

"About two am, Doctor."

"Do you…um…happen to know his first name?"

"Salman. His name was Salman Abdulaziz."

And then there was nothing to do but cover him with a sheet and make my way home, where I poured myself a strong whiskey, held the golden slippers carefully in my hand and wondered.

It had been a good story, but...woven gold? I smiled to myself as I looked at the slippers.

It was then I noticed something strange. Something you don't expect to find in slippers. I put down my glass and reached gently inside.

Sewn into each heel were several small hard objects.

*Hotel Room**

Uncertainty

Gnaws at my innards like a rat.
Stale cigar smoke
And a counterpane
Worn thin, and stained
Like my self-respect.
Still not too late

To flee, but I remain.
Time creeps on as doubt seeps in,
Congealing on my threadbare mood
Like brandy and ash on this hotel mat.
How much longer should I wait?

Ten minutes more? Twenty?
Maybe at least I'll give him that.
Maybe the traffic or the rain,
That's it! Or his children again
Maybe. What delight or pain has fate

In store for me this day?
I read once more
His letter – must make sure.
Maybe I'll discover my mistake.
'Silly you!' he'll say with kisses. Then
We'll laugh. Wrong time or place.
Maybe wrong date.

But no! Not mistaken! Foolish! How naïve,
How gullible, to think that he would leave
His wife of over twenty years for me.
How short the time between joy and grief.
How thin the line between love and hate.

Time heals, they say. Maybe. I'll tell you later.
It takes time, they say. But meanwhile
Where does all this time take me?
Time passes. This at least,
If nothing else, I can state

With some certainty.

song

*In Aleppo**

Playing football in the dust outside my home,
My brother Ahmed is in goal.
In the shadow of our apartment block we play.
This life in Aleppo,
It is the only life we know.

My mother's upstairs cooking lamb and rice and beans,
My father, he works nights, he's sleeping on the couch.
My sister Layla walking past in her new veil,
My baby brother, Abdullah,
He just likes to sit and watch.

Then I see my sister looking up,
Something moving fast, and then a flash of light.
Then I'm flying through the air
And my world turns upside down
And my day turns into night.

When they pull me from the rubble, they're all gone.
I no longer have a family, I no longer have a home.
I'm crying as I try to understand what's going on,
Why the only life I've known is over,
Why the life I knew is gone.

Then the men with beards come,
Say that I must go with them.
I'm now a soldier in their holy war,
It is Allah's will, they say.

Six months later finds me in this foreign land,
A deadly waistcoat hidden underneath my shawl.
I don't want to kill. I don't want to die.
But I no longer have a choice,
The men with beards are watching me I know.

There is a trigger hidden in my hand,
I'm a soldier in their holy war.
It is what Allah wants they say,
But I wonder, as I pull the trigger,
How can they be so sure?

*In Broad Daylight**

Where will you take me today?
My flat? With its oversized waterbed
Its planed floorboards
Smoothly rippling underfoot
Its faded cheesecloth blinds
Still sweetly redolent of
Wayward college nights
And not a cockroach in sight?

Or your studio perhaps
With its erotic bronze figurines
Cast in attitudes of fiery passion
Yet as unexpectedly cold to
The naked breast as
The Imam haranguing the faithful
At Friday prayers

And that skylight above your bed
So innocuous in sunshine
Yet peering down upon our illicit
Midnight liaisons in judgement like
The gilded ceiling mirror
In that Beirut brothel

I am sorry, my love but I was so alone
And her eyes were such dark deep pools

No! Let us return to a Suffolk meadow
One sultry August afternoon
Serenaded by clatterbuzzing dragonflies

Death and Birth and In Between

Lying on a mattress of she-loves-me
She-loves-me-not seed wool
While beneath our heads spiders
Kidnap their prey in broad daylight

I have the picnic hamper
A wicker cradle lined with crisp white napkins
Swaddling garlic chicken breasts golden and crisp
A bottle of Chardonnay chilled
One hour in the river
Smooth slices of buffalo mozzarella
And overripe beefsteak tomatoes
Juice so rich it drips from your chin like
Blood oozing surprised from a knife-wound

Garnished with the salty bite of
Anchovy-stuffed olives
Tastes contrasting as unexpectedly as
A veiled lady with an Uzi
And familiar deep dark eyes
Leaping suddenly from a
Kerb-crawling Mercedes
In broad daylight

There they are the bullrushes
Just as I remember
Heads held high
Bearded like hajjis

From a distance a group of friends
Waving farewell beside the crumbling jetty
But close up hiding the sun
Gesticulating and hostile

Now floating gently downstream
Our boat softly rocking
Cradling our hidden love
Fragile in its birth

Not just yet a return to the dark then
Linger a while on this Elysian river
As we lose our oars and are slowly and
Helplessly carried onwards
Trust me and open one last time
Beneath the passing willows
In broad daylight

No my dear there will be time enough
For my blindfold and rusting radiator
For my rats and cockroaches and flies
For the boots

Time enough

song

In Neptune's Bed[*]

It's dusk on the beach
There the lady is standing
Casting her eyes to the sea.
And the surf charges in
Like a thousand white warriors,
Hearing the prayer that she breathes.

> *Someone to love, someone to care for,*
> *Someone to show her her soul ,*
> *Someone to give, someone to live for,*
> *Someone to make her life whole.*

So the albatross wakes
To her voice like a silver dream
Singing her song to the breeze,
And the seagull is sad
As the tears trickle down her cheeks
Making their way to the sea.

> *No one to love, No one to care for*
> *No one to show her her soul*
> *No one to give, No one to live for*
> *No one to make her life whole*

> *Ding Dong the bells are ringing*
> *Somewhere under the Sea.*
> *Hear choirs of mermaids singing*
> *Summoning you to the deep.*

And she looks to the sea
And she looks to the sky
But she doesn't know which way to leap,
So she lays down her head
On the soft soft sand
And the breaking waves lull her to sleep.

Ding Dong the bells are ringing
Somewhere under the Sea.
Hear choirs of mermaids singing
Summoning you to the deep.

And the tide tiptoes in
Like a thief in the night
To steal her body away,
And the water creeps in
And the soft sand sighs,
And whispers to her as she lays:

"Lady Oh Lady
Don't Lay Down your head
Or else you'll awaken
Down in Neptune's bed."
But the Lady sleeps on
Without opening her eyes,
The words of the Seagull drowned out
By the soft sand's sighs.

It's dawn on the beach
And the tide has departed,
No trace of the lady remains
But her song echoes on
In the cry of the seagull
As she sings her lament to the rain.

Someone to love, someone to care for,
Someone to show her her soul,
Someone to give, someone to live for,
Someone to make her life whole.

And the Lady swims down
To her new home beneath the waves,
And there with the mermaids she stays,
And the sunken church bell
Slowly tolls out its message
Till another lost soul comes to pray.

Ding Dong the bells are ringing
Somewhere under the Sea.
Hear choirs of mermaids singing
Summoning you to the deep.

In the Paddock

They use a tractor now
Red and gleaming
Smugly superior
But when awake
Its voice destroys the peace
And birds fall silent
As it passes

Nearing the paddock sometimes
Just sometimes
They glance in my direction
And remember
But then turn away
In embarrassment

I tried to explain
But they wouldn't listen
A tractor is not a foal
You can't breed it
And you can't grow petrol
Like hay

I was economical really
If a bit old-fashioned

They don't visit any more
Except when the children come

And I do miss the apples

story

In the Woods

I HAD BEEN HIDING IN THE FOREST for several days. The soldiers chased me here, but didn't enter. Too scared. I was relying on that. The forest had a bad reputation, as a place where those who ventured in rarely emerged alive. It was rumoured to be haunted. I was scared too, of course I was. I had no idea what kind of creatures, earthly or supernatural, lived there. But I had no choice. This was the third time I had been caught thieving. Under the new '*Three strikes and you're out'* policy, I faced execution.

It's not that I wanted to be a thief. I had tried legit work. For a while I had been a cook, and then I tried my hand at tailoring, making cheap clothes for people in the village, I even worked as an actor in a travelling show for a while. But nothing lasted very long.

It was the taxes, always the taxes! The latest was the new War Tax, that seemed to give them the right to take whatever they wanted. To pay for the 'Special Military Intervention' in the Middle East.

I had jumped onto the back of a wagon, one of the many tax-collector's wagons that you saw about nowadays, and grabbed a bale of linen from the back. I might have got away with it too, if I hadn't tripped over the sleeping guard and woken him up.

Once I reached the forest, I ran about half a mile in then climbed up to a natural platform about 20 ft up in an ancient oak. At first I just hid quietly and waited. I wasn't sure who or what I was sharing the forest with and was terrified.

That first night it rained, and by the next morning I was soaked through to the bone. So I built a kind of shelter, using branches and leaves. I urgently needed to change my appearance so had fashioned fresh clothing from the bale of linen I had stolen. I was rather pleased with the result. It looked vaguely like a monk's habit. I stayed in the tree during the day and ventured out only at night to see what I could find to eat. By 'find' I mean steal, I didn't know how to hunt. But there was a settlement of some homeless tramps nearby and I usually managed to pick up something from them while they slept.

One evening, after I had climbed down in search of food, I felt a heavy hand on my shoulder.

"What have we here?" a deep gruff voice demanded. "Maybe you're the scoundrel who has been stealing our vittles while we sleep."

"No, No, not I!" I stammered. The owner of the voice was a huge tree trunk of a man, larger by half in all dimensions than any man had any right to be.

'So, Mr Monk, what brings you into our territory if not to steal from us or spy on us?"

I realised then that he had indeed mistaken the results of my poor needlework as a monk's habit.

"The soldiers," I blurted out, "they chased me here."

I had learned long ago that, when lying, the best policy was to include as much as possible of the truth in the lie.

"Best come with me," he said. "We'll see what the others think about you."

He led me like a dog to the encampment, where a group of ragged men were sitting round a fire roasting a huge boar on a spit.

"Who have you got there, John?" a voice called out. "It looks like you've found yourself a man of God. Are you a priest man, or a monk? Speak up. I don't recognise your order."

I thought quickly. "A travelling friar from London," I replied.

The smell of the roasting meat was in my nostrils and, to be honest, it was hard to think about anything else. I hadn't eaten for two days and the aroma was making me drool.

One of the men noticed this. "You look as if you're starving," he said. "Sit down by the fire and tuck in, friar. We can talk later."

I gratefully sat and ate my fill of the boar. One of the men passed round a flagon of wine.

After an hour or two, when everyone was dozing and I was looking around to see what I could steal, a tall man dressed in green with a bow and arrow in his hand strode into the clearing. He had a couple of rabbits slung over his shoulder.

"Who the devil is this?" he shouted. He had a loud booming voice and this annoying mannerism of slapping his thigh as he spoke.

"A travelling friar from London," my giant of a friend answered. "Found him lost in the woods about a mile away. Like the rest of us, he had run into the forest to escape the soldiers. He was starving. He ate so much of our boar that we called him Friar Tuck."

And that is how I came to join Robin Hood and his ragged men.

song

*It's Still There**

Between Hawaii and California
Lies the Great Pacific garbage patch,
But every ocean has its version of
The Great Pacific garbage patch.
Three times the size of France,
Mother Nature doesn't stand a chance.
It's where the ocean currents sweep together
All of mankind's plastic trash.

Assorted sachets of this and that,
Discarded cling film sandwich wrap,
A water bottle you left on a beach,
You know eventually the tide will reach it,
Fishing nets lost in a storm,
Still catch and kill for decades more.
Look under the surface and you'll find
That it's all still there.

> *Because every bit of plastic you put into the ocean is still there.*
> *It doesn't go away, 'cos plastic's here to stay, it's still there.*
> *Floating on the top or sinking down below,*
> *There's no plug to pull, nowhere for it to go,*
> *And everybody knows it doesn't decompose,*
> *It's still there.*
>
> *We've got to turn off the tap of plastic! Turn off the tap!*
> *Turn off the tap of plastic! Turn off the tap!*
> *We've got to stop making that stuff,*
> *We've already got far more than enough.*
> *We've got to turn off the plastic tap.*

Collected from our shores and beaches at high tide,
Lost from fishing boats or dumped overboard
From ocean liners,
Flotsam and jetsam are romantic words
But in reality they murder seals and birds,
How long will it be before everything that swims has died?

A hard hat from an oil rig,
A soft drink crate and a purple wig,
Crisp packaging you dropped overboard,
A broken doll's house, a plastic sword,
A game boy case, a drinking straw,
So many plastic bags from the corner store,
Look under the surface, and you'll find
They're all still there.

> *Because every bit of plastic you put into the ocean is still there.*
> *It doesn't go away, 'cos plastics here to stay, it's still there.*
> *Floating on the top or sinking down below,*
> *There's no plug to pull, nowhere for it to go,*
> *And everybody knows it doesn't decompose,*
> *It's still there.*

> *We've got to turn off the tap of plastic! Turn off the tap!*
> *Turn off the tap of plastic! Turn off the tap!*
> *We've got to stop putting it in,*
> *That's the only way we'll win.*
> *We've got to turn off the plastic tap.*

We used to do our shopping with paper carrier bags.
Ate fish and chips from newspaper, 'cos that's all we had.
Nets and rope from jute and hemp,
I remember camping underneath a canvas tent.
Were those traditional materials really all that bad?

Fifty years ago we put a man on the moon,
Now we watch Netflix films on our mobile phones,
We kill with remote-controlled military drones,
We got Apple watches controlling our homes.
Surely were clever enough to find
A substitute, another kind
Of material to stop our oceans from dying.

> *Because every bit of plastic you put into the ocean is still there.*
> *It doesn't go away, 'cos plastics here to stay, it's still there.*
> *Floating on the top or sinking down below,*
> *There's no plug to pull, nowhere for it to go,*
> *And everybody knows it doesn't decompose,*
> *It's still there.*
>
> *We've got to turn off the tap of plastic! Turn off the tap!*
> *Turn off the tap of plastic! Turn off the tap!*
> *We've got to stop making that stuff,*
> *We've already got far more than enough!*
> *We've got to stop putting it in*
> *That's the only way we'll win.*
> *We've got to stop it at source,*
> *That's the answer of course.*
> *We've got to turn off the plastic tap.*

song

*Joseph Stanley**

Joseph Stanley came from Barbados,
Or was it Dominica?
It's so long ago, hard to be really sure,
And there's no one left alive to ask any more,
But we know he washed up on the Liverpool shore,
An itinerant seaman, an exotic blackamoor
Around 1874.

> *He was a fish out of water, a wandering lime,*
> *A West Indian immigrant, ahead of his time.*
> *Long before the Windrush generation arrived,*
> *He was seeking adventure, his fortune to find*
> *In the soot and the grime*
> *Of Victorian England.*
>
> *Did you miss the coconuts? Did you miss the sun?*
> *Did you miss the mangos, the palm trees and the rum?*
> *Did you miss your mother? Were you the only one*
> *Who sailed away, and never returned?*

Joseph Stanley, he got married.
Sarah Ann was his bride.
They had lots of kids, it seems most of them died.
My grandfather was the oldest of those that survived.
I heard that her family were so horrified
That she'd married a black man, they'd rather she died,
They cut her off, their shame to hide.

> *Were you a fish out of water, a wandering lime,*
> *A West Indian immigrant, ahead of your time.?*
> *Long before the Windrush generation arrived,*
> *Were you seeking adventure, your fortune to find*
> *In the soot and the grime*
> *Of Victorian England?*

Did you miss the coconuts? Did you miss the sun?
Did you miss the mangos, the palm trees and the rum?
Did you miss your mother? Were you the only one
Who sailed away, and never returned?

Joseph and Sarah took in a lodger,
Cornelius was his name.
And one fateful day, those two men went to sea,
Joseph never came home, liver failure it was deemed.
Yes he died on that ship and was buried at sea,
But to wear out your liver by the age of 43
I really just can't see

He was a fish out of water, a wandering lime,
A West Indian immigrant, ahead of his time.
Long before the Windrush generation arrived,
He was seeking adventure, his fortune to find
In the soot and the grime
Of Victorian England.

Did you miss the coconuts? Did you miss the sun?
Did you miss the mangos, the palm trees and the rum?
Did you miss your mother? Were you the only one
Who sailed away, and never returned?

Now Cornelius was a huge comfort
To my great grandmama,
And within 18 months they were reading the banns,
Another wedding ring there on Sarah's fair hand.
Yet I've heard my grandfather could never understand
Just how his father died.
He didn't believe the story he'd been told.
I wish I could have asked him,
But he died when I was just ten years old.

poem

Just a slipper

I cried when I found it
Not a lot
My tears were mostly used up by then
But I still had one or two to spare

Deep under the eaves
In an old blue suitcase with black tape on the corners
Wrapped in a 1951 Daily Express
Beneath some fading black-and-white photographs
Taken when you were still young and beautiful
(I wish I'd known you when you were still young and beautiful)
One pink baby slipper trimmed with yellowing lace
A mothballed memory of first words
Of cautious steps and tumbles
Of someone younger and helpless
Who did as you wanted without argument
And needed you to care for him

Because that's what you did best
Cleaning grazed knees
Wiping tear-stained cheeks
And chasing away those evil afternoon headaches
With a rag of vinegar tied around my forehead

And later you always looked beyond
The middle-aged paunch and beard
To that red-headed freckle-faced cry-baby
And never showed the disappointment you felt
When I moved to a foreign land
And took a wife who wasn't even English

But what did you expect?
I couldn't stay a child forever
Even to please you

Towards the end you were the child
He had to feed and bathe and dress you
And later still
As you lay there crying with imaginary pains
Or real pains from imaginary wounds
I was the one that sat and held your hand
Hoping in some way to give something back
But I didn't have a vinegar rag
That could chase your demons away

I never was much use as a son really

When finally you left us we got rid of everything
It was too painful for him
Black binbags of clothes and shoes and old paste jewellery
The sediment of your life
Deposited in the Oxfam shop

And when I asked if there was anything he wanted to keep
He said with a voice that came from long ago
'Just one of her slippers'

song

*Krunchy's Final Gig**

There is greasepaint on his face,
A ginger wig upon his head,
And those far too baggy trousers
Striped with blue and white and red,
And secreted in a pocket
Hides his trademark cricket bat,
That he waves towards the audience
Should any jokes fall flat.

He wears a pink carnation
Tucked into his right lapel,
It squirts water into the eyes of kids
Who try to ring the bell
That is hanging from his trouser cord,
The children gather round
To ring his bell, get a wet face
And watch his trousers falling down.

> *We all love Krunchy.*
> *He is our favourite clown.*
> *We've laughed at him since*
> *We were little children,*
> *Krunchy's always been around.*

Standing in the wings
Sips from a hip flask full of rum,
Takes a long pull at his cigarette
Then starts to chew his thumb.
Something doesn't feel quite right,
His energy has gone,
But he owes it to his audience
He knows he must go on.

His hands have started trembling,
He is suddenly afraid,
Sweat is pouring down his forehead,
Perhaps it's just his age.
The tumbles hurt too much now,
And the bruises just won't heal,
A clown's job is really not one for
A pensioner he feels.

> *We all love Krunchy.*
> *He is our favourite clown.*
> *We've laughed with him since*
> *We were in our mothers' arms,*
> *Krunchy's always been around.*

It's time! He leaps onto the stage,
The people clap and cheer.
With his huge boots flapping wildly
No one notices his fear.
He smiles his painted smile and then
Performs a painful jig,
Then he makes one final pratfall
On his very final gig.

The audience cheer wildly,
But Krunchy doesn't stir,
And gradually the noise subsides
Till nothing can be heard.
And then the curtains close,
They kneel, remove his wig,
There's a siren in the distance,
It was Krunchy's final gig.

We all loved Krunchy
He was our favourite clown
We've laughed with him since
We were little children.
Krunchy's always been around.

We can't believe it.
The tears are running down.
We feel like we have lost a member of our family
'Cos Krunchy was our favourite clown,
And Krunchy's always been around.

story

The Last Laugh

IT WAS THE LAUGHTER that did it. Shrieking, uncontrolled, manic laughter, penetrating the fog like a skewer. The comfortable, soft fog that held me warm and close in its blanket of fluff, keeping me safe. Like a baby in his mother's arms. No, before that, like in a womb. I liked this womb. I could deal with this womb. For some reason I knew that outside the fog, the fluff, it was scary.

But the laughter, it just wouldn't stop. That manic laughter, filling my head, reaching down into this cosy womb and pulling me up.

And the smell of coffee. One of the smells, I remember a teacher telling me, in those days when I used to listen to teachers, like newly-baked bread, to have wafting round your house when someone comes round who might want to buy. Though why anyone would want to buy our place, I don't know. A real dump nowadays. Mum stopped caring once they put Dad away. Never cleaned the place. For a while she didn't even wash. That's why I got her the perfume for her birthday. Hoped it would cover her smell. But then she started showering and dolling herself up and going out in the evenings. She would never tell me where she was going. "Your Dad's not here anymore," she said once. "Someone's got to bring in the money."

When she was out one evening, I rooted around and found Dad's knife, the one he had used on that copper, in his hidey-hole. I was the only one who knew about his hidey-hole. He showed me one night when he was drunk. 'Don't tell your mother!' he said, so I didn't. The cops looked everywhere for the knife, but never found it. I keep it with me all the time nowadays. Sign of respect for the old man. No one is going to mess with me.

But the laughter! That bloody laughter. And the smell of coffee. You just can't ignore the smell of coffee. I realised that I just had to wake up and leave my comfortable fog behind.

There was another noise too. A ping, ping, ping from some kind of machine. What was that all about? Bloody annoying. And it dawned on me that I wasn't as comfortable as I had thought. I had a splitting headache, for one thing. How come I hadn't noticed it sooner? In fact, my whole body hurt. Bloody hell, what was this place?

Then there was another voice, other, that is, from that sodding laughter. Soft but strong. As if she knew what she was talking about.

"I think we need to up the morphine doctor. We need to keep him comfortable."

She was leaning over the bed fiddling with something beside me. I smelt the sweet smell of coffee on her breath. As she fiddled, something was pulling my arm, and there was a sharp pain.

"We might need to change the canula," the voice said.

Where was I? This wasn't my bed, my bedroom, I realised. There was something over my mouth too. Some sort of mask. I tried to move my arm to pull it away, but my arm didn't work anymore.

And why the hell did no one do anything about that sodding laughter?

I tried to remember, back before the laughter, before the smell of coffee, before the fog and the womb. I got back as far as school. Yes, I was walking back from school. Listening to a song by ... by ... Beefburger? No not Beefburger, something like that. Something you ate. A song about rats. Fuck! Why couldn't I think straight.

It was on a "Greatest Hits" CD I had lifted from the Paki stall in the market. The Paki saw me but didn't do anything. Never did nowadays. The first time he spotted me nicking his stuff he wagged his finger at me with his huge grin and reported me to the cops. All I got was a warning. A 13-year-old schoolboy. Underage. They can't do much, and don't really want to take on my family anyway. But I sent some of the boys round. The Demons. My boys. I liked the name. The Demons. Gives the right sort of image. No one messed with The Demons. After that he never reported me to the cops anymore. The Paki. Got all my CDs from him nowadays. I had the last laugh that time.

When my old man got locked away, I think the cops hoped that his business would just fall apart. At first Mum stepped in, did what she could for a while. Not her strength though. Better at Shepherd's Pie than shifting cannabis. So, I started helping out. No one noticed me, innocent-looking schoolboy that I was. Eventually I took over.

Where was I? Oh yes, I was listening to that Beefburger song, or whatever his fucking name was, on the Discman I had taken from that wimpy first year. Except not so wimpy. Fought back! Didn't he know who I was? Had to kick him in the bollocks before he let go. Twice. I've learned that you can hurt other kids at school as much as you like as long as it doesn't show on their face. And no kid wants to take their trousers off to show bruised bollocks to a teacher. And definitely no teacher wants a kid to take their trousers off. Nevertheless, he was tougher than I expected, the kid. Maybe in a few weeks, if he doesn't grass, I'll give him his Discman back and recruit him to the Demons. Get him to bring back the dosh to start with. Then maybe later he can start to carry the stuff round.

Meatloaf, that was the singer's name, not Beefburger, Meatloaf. The one I was listening to when ... well when it happened, whatever it was. What did happen? I was listening to the song, crossing the road when, yes, something hit me. Then I was flying through the air. After that ... nothing ... until now.

A low voice, one I recognized. My mother? Could it be? Sobbing. She asked something quietly. Pleading.

And then 'I'm sorry Mum – you're always nagging me about crossing roads, about being more careful.'

Shit! Where did that thought come from? Is that what happened? Did a car hit me while I was crossing the road? The bastard! When I find out who it was I'll send the Demons round to trash his car!

What was this place?

I felt a kiss on my forehead and smelt my mother's perfume. I recognised it. It was the one I nicked for her from John Lewis. Didn't know anything about perfumes, so just chose the most expensive one I could reach on the counter. Something number 5 it was.

Then that female voice again. "It won't be long now, Mrs Hackett. All we can do is keep him comfortable for as long as it takes."

What do they mean, "As long as it takes?" Takes to do what? What the fuck is this place?

Bat, not rat. Yes that was the name of the song by Meatloaf. Big fat scruffy bastard. Bat out of ... out of ... something or other.

Then the voices seemed to slip away. As if they were going into another room. I didn't want them to go into another room. It scared me. I tried to call out. But my mouth wouldn't work with the mask on. And my arm still wouldn't work to pull the mask away.

What was this place?

The pinging sound too started to slip away, then it stopped and was replaced by a steady constant tone, and I found myself slipping back into the fog.

And the smell of the coffee too was changing into something else. A kind of acrid burnt smell. Reminded me of that time I kicked next door's cat into the bonfire on fireworks night. Got into big trouble over that. An ugly old woman came round with a policeman. Talked about taking me away. Mum managed to convince them that it had been an accident. But we both knew it hadn't.

"He's evil, your son," the neighbour said to my mother. They were in the kitchen. Didn't know that I could hear.

"He's only nine. He doesn't know any better – he'll grow out of it," Mum said. But the neighbour just shook her head.

"Like father like son," she said. "He's just evil! I hope he rots in..." Then she noticed me standing by the kitchen door and stopped. Moved out of the area soon after.

The smell was getting stronger, the burnt smell, filling my nostrils. And the laughter. The manic, insane laughter. Getting louder and louder, filling my head, until there was nothing else.

Then I noticed other sounds. Not happy sounds. People were crying, and moaning and whimpering and screaming. It was getting hotter and hotter and I could see, even though I knew my eyes were still closed, I could see a red flickering against the darkness. Like flames. Suddenly there was this excruciating pain in my feet, as if they were burning. And my screams joined the other voices.

What was this place?

All this time the name of the song was nagging away at the back of my mind. Somehow, I felt that everything would become clear if I could just remember the name of the song.

Bat out of ...?

Bat out of ...?

Hell! That was it!

And it was then that I finally realised who it was that was laughing.

story

*Last Xmas**

THE OLD WOMAN LOOKED over her reindeer herd, smiling with satisfaction. She was wearing the traditional red and white Father Xmas outfit with matching red and white hat. That's what they expected, the children. And their parents. Dozens of them came every day. Flew in from the south of Finland, but also from Russia and Sweden and further afield. This year there had even been few visitors from England. They came for the famous *Santa and Reindeer Experience*. The old woman wore a badge which said, in several languages, *Santa's Little Helper*. The family reindeer herd was her trump card, the advantage she had over her competitors. The sleigh-rides through the forest pulled by her reindeer were a great success.

She wondered how many more years they would be able to continue. She had noticed that Jyrki, her husband, who had dressed as Santa for the last twenty years, had been drunk several times this year while working. He maintained that his breath didn't smell after drinking vodka, but the parents were beginning to notice. One snooty German woman actually complained about it. And it would only take one or two bad reviews, she knew, and the visitors would start going elsewhere. You can't have a Xmas experience business with an alcoholic Santa. Maybe this would have to be their last Xmas.

She turned back to the reindeer, who were all enthusiastically nibbling away at moss under the snow, and did her customary headcount. From tomorrow onwards she would allow them to roam free again to find their own food. And she would take away the tinsel and baubles from their antlers. And wash away the red food colouring they had put on the nose of one of them. The children expected that as well.

Head count complete – all present and correct – she turned back the house. This far north it was dark of course, although not completely black, the luminosity of the thick snow reflecting the starlight and the quarter moon. It was a couple of months since she had last seen the sun, and even then it had been only a brief glimpse on the horizon before fading again. Now, at Xmas, there was just a slight glow on the skyline in the middle of the day showing whereabouts it was hiding.

One of the reindeer was behaving strangely, she noticed, the one with the red nose – a bit frisky, she thought, lifting his head and glancing from side to side as if looking for something. Ah well, never mind, she'll check on him in the morning. She closed the gate to ensure they were all secure and made her way back to the house. The fence wouldn't keep the wolves out, of course, but Blixen, her old dog, would bark a warning if they approached.

She opened the door and stepped inside. She was glad to be able to take off the Father Xmas outfit, which itched and seemed to get tighter every year, and change back into her usual jeans and baggy sweatshirt. She looked into Ilkka's bedroom as she passed. Ilkka was her fourteen-year-old grandson. He was playing on the new computer game he had received as a present that afternoon. She didn't dare tell him it was time to sleep. The last time she had done that he had sworn at her. She shook her head, wondering what would become if him.

Jyrki was snoring on the sofa. When they had first started the business he had embraced the role of Santa enthusiastically, even growing his grey beard long for it. Now his beard was white and, she saw, stained around the mouth by food and cigarettes. She noticed he had knocked a photograph off the sideboard and bent down to pick it up. Why couldn't Jyrki take more care? It was the only picture she had of her grandmother, her mother's mother, and was valuable to her.

She remembered her Nan snorting at the benign, fat, rosy-cheeked Santa Claus that Coca Cola had given the world. Every year she would make the same complaint.

"Saint Nick isn't jolly," she used to say, "and he isn't fat. And he certainly doesn't wear red and white."

"How do you know, Nan?" the children asked, never tiring of hearing the same story.

"Because I saw him once, when I was very young," she said.

"So, what did he look like?" they would ask.

Nan would always lean close and speak in a low voice, looking around in case anyone else should hear. "He was tall and thin," she said, "and wasn't jolly at all but serious, a bit scary really, and wore green not red."

"And did he have horns?" one of her cousins asked.

"No, not Saint Nick, no." She looked serious now. "He didn't have horns. But there was this other one who followed him around. He was really frightening. And he *did* have horns on his head. He looked like a kind of goat. Or a demon. Or maybe a cross between the two. Santa called him *Krampus.*

"Why did Krampus follow Santa?" the children would always ask.

"Well, you see, Santa was the one who gave presents to the children who had been good that year."

She always paused at this point and knocked back a shot of *Koskenkorva*, the local vodka.

"And Krampus, well, it was his job to punish the children who had been naughty."

"So how did you meet him, Nan?"

"One year, on Xmas eve, I was asleep when I heard a noise. I crept out onto the landing and there they were, Krampus and St Nick. Arguing. About me. About whether I had been good or bad that year. I saw them. I laid perfectly still – I didn't want them to know I was awake. Though it was really scary." At this point in the story she usually poured herself another shot of *Koskenkorva*.

"It was a hell of a row," she said. "But St Nick was big and strong and Krampus seemed, well, smaller and intimidated by him. Anyway, St Nick won and Krampus left in a temper."

And the children would always sit in silence picturing the scene.

The old woman replaced the photograph on the sideboard. She hadn't thought about her Nan for many years. She suddenly realised how much she missed her. And those strange stories she used to tell. All vodka-fuelled rubbish of course, but she missed her Nan all the same.

Death and Birth and In Between

* * *

Later, when all was quiet in the house and the other reindeer were asleep, and the dog gently snoring in his kennel, the frisky reindeer, the one with the red food-colouring on his nose, walked silently to the gate and leaped over. Or rather, maybe leaped isn't the right word. He seemed to fly over. To rise up and glide over. He landed on the other side and stepped carefully towards the small area of forest nearby.

A figure detached itself from the shadows and stepped forward. He was skinny and gaunt, and very, very old, walking with great difficulty with the help of a crooked cane. He was dressed in a grubby green and white tunic and had his hood raised covering his bald head. A filthy white beard was just visible beneath his tunic.

"You took your time, Rudy," he said.

The reindeer just looked at him.

"OK, OK, I know you've got to be careful."

They walked together through the forest until they came to a clearing where there was an ancient, battered sleigh. It was almost empty, just a few parcels wrapped in paper and green ribbon tied in a bow laying in the bottom.

"Are you sure you can still do this?" the man asked. "After all, there's just the one of you now."

The reindeer didn't answer, just looked at him for a second then stepped forward until he was positioned between the harnesses.

"Do you remember when there was a dozen of you?" the old man asked, his voice cracking. "Now you're the only one. All the others just got too old and died. Donner was the last. He went last year. And there don't seem to be any more coming through with the flying thing. Recessive gene I suppose."

He glanced at the reindeer out of the corner of his eye.

"I don't suppose you've fathered any young uns this year, have you?"

The reindeer didn't answer.

The old man shook his head. "Now it's just you and me Rudy. Do you remember when the sleigh was piled high with presents for all the children?"

He shook his head again.

"They don't need us anymore. They've got too many toys already nowadays. The magic just isn't there. You've got to believe in magic for it to work, and the kids today, well, they've got no belief," he said sadly. "And the fewer kids believe in us, the harder it is, the older and weaker we get. That's the way it works. And nowadays," he said shaking his head, "There aren't many children who have been good enough over the year for us to visit even if they do believe."

He tied the reindeer to the harnesses.

"And do you remember when old Krampus was around, ready to punish the naughty ones? Haven't seen him for ages. Ever since we had that row, do you remember, over that little girl? Come to think of it she lived round here somewhere, I think. She had been telling lies, but only to protect her brother, he was the naughty one. Krampy said a lie is a lie, but I wouldn't let him have her. Hell of a row that was. Wonder what he's been doing with himself recently?"

He clambered onto the sleigh with much grumbling and cursing at the effort.

"I wonder who'll last longest," he said, "you or me old thing?"

The reindeer didn't answer, just waited.

"Come on then we might as well get started."

Rudolph lifted his front hooves and started pulling the sleigh. It was a lot of effort and he could hardly get it moving at all. He was struggling. At one point he lay down in the thick snow and didn't move for several seconds. The old man thought he might have to give up. But then he climbed to his feet again and laboriously dragged the sleigh to the edge of the clearing and turned. He stood there for what seemed like an eternity. Then, with a snort, determination in his eyes, he charged forward as fast as he could and finally, first the reindeer, then the sleigh lifted a few inches off the ground. Straining with the effort he aimed at a gap where the trees were lowest and finally they were through and out of the forest and lifting into the night sky. They circled above the farmhouse twice then headed south.

"You know, I think this may well have to be our last Xmas," the old man said.

* * *

When they were safely out of sight, another figure detached himself from the shadows. He stood tall and straight, his chest and shoulders sleek and smooth, his legs hairy, his horns polished, glinting in the starlight. No feebleness or frailty here. He was strong and powerful, and getting stronger every year. It was a very, very, naughty world.

He turned and made his way to the house, stopping for a moment at the door and listening, before continuing round the side until he came to a window. This was the place where he and the old man had fought over that little girl. Where the old man had humiliated him in front of her. She had been hiding at the top of the stairs, but Krampus had smelt her there. She was long dead of course, but it was the same family living in the same cottage. He had unfinished business here.

He had been waiting all this time in the forest, growing in strength. They had forgotten about him, the children. Forgotten that you can't have good without bad, light without dark, presents without punishment. He had been neglecting his duties, but now he was back. He would start here and then, well, there were a lot of children on his list.

From the reflection in the glass he could see that someone inside wasn't asleep and was playing a computer game. He smiled a goatish grin, reached up and levered the window open.

story

Like a Child

"WHAT YOU NAME?" she asked as she gave him his beer. "Where you from?"

Stock questions learned long before the girls have acquired enough English to fully understand the answers.

He took a couple of sips nervously and looked around. It was still early and the clutch of open girlie bars for which this area of Phuket was known was largely empty. A few girls were sitting behind their counters fixing make-up, and one or two foreign men, *farang* as the Thais call them, were drinking beer and looking bored, but the evening had not yet really started, the few girls who were already working by far outnumbering the customers. Each time a *farang* walked in, they came to life, "Welcome!", "You come my bar!" "Sit down here mister!" in friendly competition with each other, girl against girl, bar against bar, as always.

The girl behind the counter was looking up at him expectantly.

"Richard," he said, remembering the question. "And I come from England." Then he smiled, only now actually looking at her for the first time. "What's your name?"

"Dim," she replied.

He suppressed a smile. "How long have you worked here?"

She concentrated. "Eleven day."

"And before?"

"I sell gasoline."

He looked her up and down. "How old are you?"

"Twenty-two."

"No," he said, "You look younger."

She tossed her head angrily. He realised he had touched a sore spot.

"Twenty-two!" she said, "Sure!"

Death and Birth and In Between

She reached under the counter and took out a Connect 4 game. They started to play.

"Why do you work in a bar?" he asked her.

"I send money me family. Mama, Papa, baby."

"Your baby?"

"Yes." She looked sad for a moment. "Baby ... stay me Mama. I send money. Mama ... care ... she." Her English was broken and inaccurate, punctuated by frequent pauses as she searched for the correct word, but just about adequate. She looked him in the eyes.

"You have baby? Madam?"

He took some photographs from his wallet; they showed a tall blonde woman in a studio pose, flanked by two tall, blonde, teenage boys, obviously twins. "This is my wife," he said, "and these are my sons."

She laughed with delight, calling some other girls over, and for a few minutes they pored over the pictures excitedly. He took the chance to study her. She had long, dark hair, thick, worn in a waved style unusual among Thais, drawn back from a strongly sloping forehead. She had high cheekbones and a long nose. She was not beautiful, but her appearance was striking and unusual. And appealing.

She handed back the pictures, which he put in his wallet quickly.

"Would you like a drink?" he asked.

She smiled at him and nodded, then called to one of the other girls, who brought her a gin and tonic. Girls weren't paid to work in this kind of place, he knew, they were expected to make their money through private arrangements with customers, although Richard didn't have the faintest idea how that side of things worked. But he knew that she would get 40 or 50 Baht if he bought her a drink. And that the 'lady drink' would cost him twice as much as his own.

Sitting opposite Dim, playing Connect 4, he found himself quietly taken in by her unusual looks and innocent charm.

"Where did you learn your English?" he asked.

"Have book," she said. "And have app me iPhone." She took out her phone and showed it to him, but the Thai script was just meaningless squiggles to him. "Every morning I study…one hour before I working."

"And you have learned so much in just eleven days?"

She laughed, "Customer speaking English. If I no can word, I ask…" she concentrated for a moment, "some lady help."

* * *

Over a beer the following day, he was talking to Doug, an Australian expat who was staying at the same guesthouse. Doug was one of those bar stalwarts so common in Thailand, beer constantly in hand, who never lets lack of knowledge prevent him from giving an authoritative opinion.

"So did you take her back to your room?" Doug asked.

Richard's cheeks reddened slightly. "No, I … that isn't why I went there … It's just a nice place to find company where you're travelling alone and you don't know anyone in a place. It's worth the price of a drink or two." He paused for a moment. "How does it work then?" His cheeks were going even redder, "Getting a girl to go with you?"

"Easy!" Doug took another swig of his beer. "You just ask her, straight out. That's what they expect. If she likes the look of you, she'll agree. It's best to discuss then and there how much you will pay her. She will ask you if you want short time or long time."

"What does that mean?" Richard asked.

"Short time is just an hour or two … back to your room … boom boom … back to the bar again. Long time you spend the night together and have a second crack at her in the morning."

Richard felt quite disgusted with the way Doug explained things, but he was well aware that this attitude was normal for the hordes of western men who come to Thailand looking for sex. As he had never seen Doug anywhere else except propping up the bar, beer in his hand, morning till night, he wondered if he had really ever managed to gain first-hand experience of what he was describing.

"Then you pay something to the bar, a bar fine they call it," Doug continued. "You're paying the bar because the girl isn't there working while she's out with you."

"But the bar doesn't pay her anyway."

Doug smiled. "I know, mate. Either free labour from the girls, or money from the *farang*. It's the bar owner who wins every which way."

As he was turning to leave, Doug called after him. "Hey, mate, you got any rubbers?"

By now Richard's face was beetroot. "No, that's not why I came…"

Doug reached into his bag, and tossed him a couple of condoms. "Passed their use-by date, mate," he said, "but should still be good for a quickie!"

* * *

That evening he went initially to a different bar and drank several beers. However, he found his thoughts continually being drawn back to Dim, and inevitably his legs followed his thoughts and he returned. It was later than the night before and as he entered the street, he was struck by the cacophony of competing music systems and constant shouting as the bars vied with each other to attract custom. There were more customers than the previous evening, mostly male and mostly *farang*, but more girls as well and they still seemed to outnumber the customers.

His heart gave a little flutter when he saw Dim again. It was a feeling he recognised, but had not felt since adolescence.

When she saw him, she gave a broad, genuine smile, a half-moon revealing slightly uneven teeth which would have been straightened back home, but which added character to her smile and gave her face charm.

"You come back!" she said. "I think you no like me!"

"No, No!" he went red again, "I mean, yes, I do like you."

She smiled her uneven smile again, and her eyes were laughing at his embarrassment. She knew he had come back for her and was flattered. She tossed her head as they spoke, and wrinkled her nose in a way that made his neck tingle.

"You want drink?" she asked.

"Not now," he said. He realised he was slightly drunk. He took a deep breath. "Do you want to come back to my room with me?"

She looked at him for several seconds before answering. "OK, but I go you long time!" she said," I no go short time. You give me…" she paused for a moment, whether to find the right words, or to assess how much she thought she could get him to pay, he couldn't tell. "Two thousand Baht, OK?"

It was over the odds, he knew from his discussions with Doug, but when he translated it back into English money, the difference didn't seem important.

"Yes, OK," he said. "But my holiday finishes on Saturday. That's when I fly back to England. So I would like you to stay with me until Friday. That's three days."

She looked up at him with wide eyes, and tried to find the right words. "Wow!" she said.

He paid the bar fine and she went off to collect her things. Before leaving he saw her buy a small garland from a street vendor, place it over a picture of Buddha, which served as the bar shrine, and say a small quiet prayer. The devotion was unobtrusive and he found it touching.

Now that she was no longer sitting on the bar stool, he was surprised to see how tiny she was. Many Thai girls are small, but she was diminutive, almost like a child. As she took his arm, she asked bluntly, "You have condom?"

"Yes," he replied, grateful that Doug had insisted on giving them to him.

"Good," she said. "Thai condom no good."

* * *

They went out for a meal then back to the guesthouse. He was worried that the owner would question him about bringing a girl back, but it seemed perfectly normal, expected even. They did ask to see her ID though, and she had to sign in a book at reception.

In bed, he was nervous and clumsy and realised he maybe should have drunk fewer beers. It was the first time he had had sex with anyone other than his wife since long before they were married, over twenty years earlier. And Dim was disappointingly unresponsive, lying there, motionless, staring at the ceiling. Afterwards, lying together, he stroked her hair and kissed her gently on the neck.

"It will be better tomorrow," he said. "I won't have any beer tomorrow."

She turned to him. "You good man," she said. "You good heart." They lay in silence for a while.

"Tell me about your family," he asked.

"I no live Papa home," she said, "I live home ... husband."

He was taken aback. "You mean you are married?"

"No more. I have husband before, yes, but no more." She paused trying to find the right words. "I marry three year but he no good. He drink too much. He like lady too much. He butterfly! I want finish but him no want. So I come Phuket." She was getting animated. "He no work. I work sell gasoline. He take money and ..." she couldn't find the right words. "Drink! Lady! Too much lady! He no good! No good!"

"Your husband. Does he know where you are?"

"No. I no tell."

"Do your parents know?" She looked at him confused. He tried again. "Mama, Papa, they know?"

"They know I come Phuket." She hesitated. "They no know I work bar. I say them I work restaurant."

"Do you send them money?"

She nodded. "I send half. Half is me."

"Don't send them too much money," Richard said, "Or they will guess."

She looked thoughtful. "I think Papa know, but I no tell. Maybe tell after."

* * *

The following morning he went down to find some breakfast. He left Dim sleeping in his room. Bar girls usually work until 2 am and then sleep until midday.

He found Doug in his normal spot, his usual beer exchanged for a black coffee.

"Don't get sweet on her!" Doug warned Richard. "All these Thai girls want is to get themselves a *farang* husband. They'll say anything, or do anything to make it happen." He laughed. "I knew one bloke, here for several months he was, who fell for this girl. Wanted to marry her. We thought he knew the score. Thing is, she wasn't a lady at all, she was *katoey*, a ladyboy." Doug laughed. "He was a virgin when he came to Thailand. He'd been screwing her but she'd had the operation and he didn't know what a pussy ought to look like. When he started talking about marriage, we told him, of course. He didn't believe us at first." Doug finished his coffee and ordered a beer. "It was only when she stayed the whole night with him, and he noticed the stubble in the morning that he finally believed us." He looked at Richard. "These Thai girls will lie through their teeth to get their claws into you. So, you be careful, mate. Don't get sweet on her!"

* * *

Later, when she finally surfaced, Richard suggested going to the beach.

"But I no have..." She mimed a swimming costume.

"No problem," he said, "I buy you one."

When they went into the shop, he started making his way towards the womenswear department, but she pulled him back.

"No! No!" she said, and led him instead to the children's department where she easily found a swimsuit to fit.

They went to the beach and sat down on deck chairs, under a huge sunshade. He opened his novel and started reading. She was looking at a comic.

An elderly German woman on their left, slowly roasting in the sun, started looking at him with an expression of undisguised contempt. He was surprised. *Farang* men with Thai girlfriends were not that uncommon a sight here. He ignored her and went back to his book.

Death and Birth and In Between

After a few minutes he became aware of an extremely sunburned English family on his right muttering and glancing in his direction. The children were asking something, and the mother was getting flustered trying not to answer their questions directly. He caught a fragment of what she was saying though, and suddenly his faced flushed with embarrassed understanding.

He stood up quickly. "Come!" he said, "We're going."

She followed without question, but back in the guesthouse she asked, "What is problem?"

"Can I see your ID please?"

She nodded, retrieved her card from her bag, and handed it to him obediently. It was all in Thai script of course, which he was unable to read, but there were some numbers on it, which he did understand.

"Does it show your birthday anywhere?" he asked.

Again she nodded and pointed to a date: twenty-five thirty-four, the Buddhist era having started five hundred years before ours.

"And what year is it now?"

She took her comic from her bag and pointed at a top corner. Twenty-five fifty-six. He calculated rapidly, then gave a sigh of relief. She had been telling the truth – she really was twenty-two years old.

"What is problem?" she asked again.

"Those people on the beach were talking," he said. "They think I am a … He stopped and tried again, choosing simple words. "They think you child. They think I bad man who go with child…" He swallowed. It was a difficult thing for him to say. "They think I bad man who want sex with child. You understand?"

"But I no child!" she said, her eyes flashing. "I twenty-two! I marry three year!"

"I know he said, "But you are small. They think you are child."

"They stupid!" she said and tossed her head indignantly.

***

That night he found the sex easier. He managed not to think of his wife, and Dim was much more responsive. Their love-making was long and slow and, at least for his part, truly wonderful.

But afterwards, she gave a squeal of dismay, and when he looked down, he discovered that the condom had broken, and in their passion neither of them had noticed. And, lying in bed in the dark afterwards, whereas the night before had seen gentle, intimate pillow talk, there was only worried awkwardness. It was a new and disquieting situation for both of them. He didn't think he had much to fear from her – she had only been a bargirl for less than a fortnight – but she was scared. So, he embraced her and stroked her hair, reassuring her gently. He decided to try and take her mind off what had happened.

"Do you like be bargirl?" he asked. He was amused to notice that he had started speaking in the same broken simplified English she used.

She thought for a long while before replying. "I no like ... occupation." She paused for a while, thinking. "I like boom-boom ... sometimes ... tonight you boom-boom good, but ... sometime no good." Then she turned to him and laughed. "But I like money customer give!"

"How long you think you work bar?"

Instead of answering, she raised herself onto one elbow and looked him in the eyes. "You ask question too much," she said. "Why?"

He wanted to explain that most tourists who come to Thailand don't see much beyond the beach, restaurant and hotel. They never learn anything about the realities of life in Thailand, never try to find out what Thai people are thinking behind the ubiquitous smile, never get any deeper into Thai culture than their first green curry. Speaking to her, he could discover something about her life, her thoughts. He had a window into her country, into her culture. Not a large window, admittedly, and maybe through that window he was seeing only a tiny and unrepresentative fragment of Thai life, but it was a window nonetheless. Of course, he found it impossible to express these thoughts in words she could understand, so he said simply,

"I want understand you life."

She accepted this simplistic explanation.

"One year I want have…"

She paused, then reached for her phone and typed in a number and showed it to him.

"Three hundred thousand Baht?"

She repeated the number carefully.

"Yes, I want three hundred thousand Baht. I want buy land for house. I pay already six thousand Baht." He did a quick conversion. Three hundred thousand Baht was about six thousand pounds. And, he realised, a tall order in just a year if what he was paying her was typical. Especially if she was sending half to her parents.

"Your life … can be dangerous," he said awkwardly. "Have you had any problems with unpleasant men?" But she didn't understand. He tried again. "You no have problem bad man?"

"No." she said, "Good man, same same you. Man with good heart." He told her to be careful, but she was dismissive. "I no go bad man!" she said, as if you could always accurately judge character from the other side of a Connect 4 board.

* * *

The next day she showed him, with disturbingly childlike excitement, her collection of foreign coins.

"This one Australia," she said, eyes alive. "He give me tip one thousand Baht at airport. And this one Hong Kong. And this Sweden. He buy me shoes. This one man German. He drink too much, no can boom-boom, but give me much present. And this one black man America. He good heart but…" she grimaced, "He too big." She turned to Richard. "You give England coin me?"

He gave her a 50p coin, his heart sinking as he realised that there were far too many coins in her collection for just eleven days of bar work. He realised too, with sadness, that this was probably all she would remember about him. Maybe for a few days the subject of bargirl laughter in idle moments. "First night banana no work … too much beer. But second night him better," or "Condom break. He say me no problem, but I worry." But soon her memory of him would be overlaid by more recent faces, more recent bodies, and probably more importantly, more recent presents. Maybe she would remember him for a while for the swimsuit he bought her, or the new English words he taught her. Eventually, though, he would be little more than a coin in her collection.

He was shocked to realise how much these thoughts upset him. She was a dream and he didn't want to wake up. Yet that was how it should be. He had a wife at home, after all. And you have to wake up from dreams.

When their three days were up he paid her what they had agreed, added far too large a tip, and put her on a motorcycle taxi back to her bar. He wanted to tell her to find a *farang* to care for her, to marry her, to take her away. Part of him wanted to do it himself, but he knew of course that that was impossible. He wanted to say 'Find him quick, before you are jaded and hardened by the life you lead. Find him before the money becomes too addictive. Find him before you choose poorly and get yourself raped or beaten by a bad man who doesn't have a 'good heart'. Find your *farang* before your spirit is damaged, before your petals drop, and your colour and bloom fade. Find him before sickness takes you. Find him before you become ... before you become like all the others.'

But he didn't of course, and was silent as the taxi sped away, and sadder than he should have been.

***

"You've got to be very unlucky," Doug said, "Even if the bloody thing did break. I read somewhere there's only one chance in a thousand of catching HIV after just one time. Or was it a million? Can't bloody remember." He laughed. "Even if she is infected. You've got to screw her lots and lots of times to be in any real danger." He took a swig of beer. "You know, the girls are worried about us *farang* men. They're told that we are the ones who give them AIDS. But it's the Thai men who are the real problem. They go with prostitutes all the time, not like the bargirls here, but nasty, dirty places." He turned his head away and looked into the distance for a moment. "Last year a brothel burned down in Pattaya, and they found the bodies of several girls afterwards who were chained to their beds. Now that's bloody nasty!" He took another swig of beer. "Thai men don't like to wear anything, either, then they catch an itch, come home, and give it to their wives. That's where the real problem is. Nah mate, I don't think you've got anything to worry about."

* * *

Richard slept for much of the flight back, and when he woke up he realised he had been dreaming of her, and reliving moments of their short time together. He smiled and felt a pang of regret. She would always have a small place in his heart. She was a secret memory that he would take out once in a while when alone and cherish.

Yet later, in the immigration queue at Heathrow, he thought for an instant he saw her face, nose wrinkled, smiling at him with her crooked smile. But when he rushed over, it wasn't her, of course, it was a young girl who held tightly to her mother's hand for protection, while her mother scowled him away.

At first, reunited with his wife and family, and plunged back into the maelstrom of day-to-day life, he managed to push her from his mind. And for a few months that summer he hardly thought of her at all. But the following winter, when the first real symptoms of his illness became evident, he knew then that he would have cause to remember her for the rest of his life.

But he didn't blame her. Not for an instant. How could he?

She was so like a child.

song

Living Alone

Living alone, is not what it seems,
I gain back my freedom, but give up my dreams.
While all of that freedom is not so much fun.
Sleeping with strangers, but waking alone.

Sleeping alone in a king-sized bed,
Plenty of pillows but only one head.
I reach out at night, just a pillow to hold,
My memories are boiling, but my body is cold.

> *If I could turn back time and do things again,*
> *I would try harder to stay your best friend.*
> *I'd nurture your spirit, stroke your hair when you cried,*
> *If I could go back to the day before our love died.*

Eating alone is never much fun,
When I'm in the market, I'm buying for one.
I don't lay the table, I don't see the need,
A takeaway pizza beside the TV.

> *If I could turn back time and do things again,*
> *I would try harder to stay your best friend.*
> *I'd nurture your spirit, stroke your hair when you cried,*
> *If I could go back to the day before our love died.*

Lollypop

yesterday I was a lollypop
licked all over
your eyes closed in ecstasy
sticky sweet on your tongue

tomorrow maybe a gobstopper
nestling in your mouth
as you suck gently
dissolving in your saliva

today I am a cream cake
squirting carelessly over your breast
as you bite into me
leaving a white moustache on your lip
and a hint of strawberry on your tongue

I want you to consume me
with lips and tongue and teeth
to devour me
until I have nothing left to give

but for now I wait patiently
for you to desire me again
like when I was a lollypop

Mantra

searching
for that place
where I can hide
from the chattering

deeper and deeper
over and over
round and round
the rhythm of my breath
the rhythm of my heartbeat
the rhythm of my mantra

the stillness just out of reach
the chatter of the world fading
into the darkness behind
but not yet gone

distantly aware of the cave
distantly aware of them shaking me
distantly aware of their voices
"...Four days now"
"...hardly beathing"
"...no food or drink..."
not yet deep enough

a light appears ahead
I know now
I can never stop
retreating deeper still
towards the stillness
towards the silence
towards the light
just out of reach

Death and Birth and In Between

poem

Miss Perkins takes Early Retirement

The teacher at the whiteboard turns to face
Her class. A snigger from the boy beside
The window, causes her to lose her stride
And stammer trying not to meet his gaze.
Accusingly he stares at her. Today
He knows, but how? They were discreet, she saw
To that. They left unseen – the hotel Doorman
Sneered, but took her coins and closed one eye.
She freezes, cannot say a word. The silence
In the classroom seems to last for ever.

The voice inside her head destroyed with guilt
Defences that a lifetime's fears had built.

song

The Morning After[*]

It's morning time,
I open just one weary eye and look around.
Sun pours through the window
Like a pool of butter spreading on the ground.
Bird outside my window singing cheerfully
I wish he'd go away.
My head is throbbing painfully, I realise
That I am really not quite ready for the day.

Oh, oh, oh, oh.

But then my eyes both open wide
Because I see with some surprise
There's someone lying next to me.
The pillow holds a cloud of hair,
Head turned away, one shoulder bare
Just wonder who the hell is she.

Oh, oh, oh, oh.

> *Cast my mind back,*
> *Concentrate!*
> *Just can't remember*
> *Who's this lying next to me.*
> *Might I? Could I? Did I? Would I?*
> *God!! I hope I didn't,*
> *Who the hell is she?*

Oh, it must have been a hell of a party,
Wonder was I good or bad,
Wonder what the hell it was I had.

It must have been a hell of a party,
I just hope I didn't say
Too many things that I'll regret today.

It must have been a hell of a party,
Bra and pants upon the chair,
Trousers in the corner over there.

It must have been a hell of a party,
Wonder what I did and said
And I wonder who is this I've got in bed.

> *Cast my mind back,*
> *Concentrate!*
> *Just can't remember*
> *Who's this lying next to me.*
> *Might I? Could I? Did I? Would I?*
> *God!! I hope I didn't,*
> *Who the hell is she?*

Tiptoe to the door
To get some aspirin and water,
Then stare quietly till I am sure,
I've never ever seen that face before.
So then I tiptoe back to bed
And quietly lay down my head,
I close my eyes and try to get some sleep
Then maybe I'll remember things.

Then there's a movement of the sheets,
And the sound of quiet feet,
Then she's opening the door,
Then the sound of running water,
Then she's gathering her clothes,
But I just keep my eyes closed.

Then I feel soft lips upon my cheek,
And the sound of moving feet,
And the front door as she leaves.
A silence that is deep and long,
The bird has finished with his song,
And I can feel the sun has gone,
And I feel a little sad,
And I wish I'd said goodbye.

song

*My Dylanesque Song**

I go back alone
To a place that isn't home
With no lover to phone
Just a silent ringtone
Got my emotions on loan
So I try to get stoned
But I've got no one to get high for

In the dark of the night
I wake up with a fright
Dreams of shadows that bite
Something's wrong it's not right
Round my throat something tight
And my hand can't feel the light
But I've nobody to die for

And then waking at dawn
With my fantasised porn
My body like a unicorn
With its impudent horn
When reality's torn
And all hope is stillborn
But I've got nobody to sigh for

So I take on the day
Anaesthetising the pain
Like a moth in the flame
Or an unsanitised drain
Or an unexplained stain
On a cracked window pane
'Cos I've got nobody to cry for

Then again home alone
Like a dog without a bone
Still got no one to phone
And my hair is uncombed
And my whiskers have grown
And I weigh twenty stone
I've just got nobody to try for

I just sit here and wait
Drinking beer by the crate
Fish and chips from a dirty plate
Watching TV till late
Wondering how to get a date
In a world full of hate
When I've got nobody to fight for

I remember the day
Where I kind of lost my way
In a whiskey-soaked daze
And she chose not to stay
Didn't like the way I played
Through that smoke-filled haze
That was itching her eyeballs

A man once wrote *Lay Lady Lay*
And the *Sad Eyed Lady*
Of the Lowlands and hey
That one about the *Slow Train*
Coming, but what's in a name
And would his songs still sound the same
If he were still called Robert Zimmerman?

So this song is a wrap
Although some of the lyrics are crap
Hope my shoulder won't feel a tap
From the policeman in the hat
In charge of poetry and rap
Closing the handcuffs with a snap
Saying this song is disrespectful

Time to finish this song
Before it gets too long
And the words start going wrong
Cos the rhymes aren't that strong
They burn like coals in hot tongs
In my Dylanesque song
That I've got nobody to sing to

song

Nobody Sees[*]

Old man in Waterloo station
His clothes are all ragged and worn
Soles of his shoes are newspaper
His fingers are blistered and torn
And his eyes full of nothing
But sorrow and suffering
He can't remember his name
No traces of pride can remain
In a life full of pain
So he drinks it away with a bottle a day
Of a liquid that's driving him blind
He is stoking the fires in his mind
While his body decays

> *Nobody looks Nobody sees*
> *Nobody wants to catch his disease*
> *Nobody tries Nobody cares*
> *We all close our eyes*
> *And pretend he's not there*
>
> *As you walk down the street*
> *You look down at your feet*
> *And pretend he's not there*
> *The authorities say*
> *"You've got nowhere to stay*
> *We'll pretend you're not there"*
> *And the police will tell*
> *him he can't go to jail*
> *"It's too good for you there!"*

He takes from his pocket a bottle
Of sweet methylated decay
Pours it through teeth that are rotten
And lips that are blistered and stained

Death and Birth and In Between

There's a tap on his back
As the I'm alright jack-booted
Policeman says he must away
To his supper of garbage and
Bedroom of dustbins and drains
So he lays down to sleep
On his mattress of concrete
And hopes that tonight it won't rain
That's another day over
Another day fewer of pain

> *Nobody looks Nobody sees*
> *Nobody wants to catch his disease*
> *Nobody tries Nobody cares*
> *We all close our eyes*
> *And pretend he's not there*
>
> *As you walk down the street*
> *You look down at your feet*
> *And pretend he's not there.*
> *The authorities say*
> *"You've got nowhere to stay*
> *We'll pretend you're not there"*
> *And the police will tell*
> *him he can't go to jail*
> *"It's too good for you there!"*

*Not A Love Song**

There are far too many love songs written
This you can't deny
Songs of love discovered and love lost
Love born and love that's died
Songs of love that's unrequited
Love that dare not speak its name
So what with all these love songs
I hope you will not blame me
If this song is not a love song
I'm going to sing it all the same

They say love is like insanity
All that ecstasy and pain
But although I've had my crazy moments
Nowadays I'm sane
So I'll leave love songs to the young to sing
And now that I'm old and grey
I won't be writing love songs
On this or any other day
I've got no time for love songs
No matter what you say

> Yet when I walk behind you
> Along that foreign street
> And you're playing your accordion
> To everyone you meet
> I see real music bring them joy
> There's laughter in their eyes
> And I get a warm warm feeling
> Growing somewhere deep inside me
> But this song is not a love song
> I truly hope you're not surprised

I write songs about those issues
About which I'm most concerned
Like plastic in the oceans
And why that tower block burned
Like prejudice and homelessness
Corruption and deceit
Why children have to die in warfare
Poisons in the food we eat
I've got no time for love songs
Surely you can see

 Yet when I see you flying down
 The hillside on your bike
 A crazy grin slapped on your face
 Hair streaming out behind
 Just like a teenage girl
 And I find my eyes are wet
 Please don't mistake this for a love song
 I hope you won't forget
 That I've got no time for love songs
 As I've already said

Sometimes I'll tell a story
In the lyrics that I write
On someone else's life and cares
I hope to shine a light
A dying clown a down-and-out
A prostitute a thief
My mother with dementia
My daughter's birth in brief
I've got no time for love songs
Surely you can see

Yet when I come upstairs
to the bedroom as you sleep
Bringing you your morning tea
I sometimes kiss your cheek
Often I'll just stop and stare
Maybe I'll stroke your head
Surely this can't be a love song
Unless I have misled you
So if this is not a love song
It must be something else instead

Ode to a Peppermill

you crouch on the cloth
squat as a mushroom
glowering awash
with resentment replete
with wizened seeds
like diminutive walnuts
or black shrunken heads
lying cratered and wrinkled
by age and disease
in an African market

now making your move
black beret over eyes
your skin marble-smooth
you've shed inhibition
rotating your body
alluring yet decadent
promising spice
and tongue-tip tingling
tastes of sin
exotic but naughty
erotic but nice
shamelessly yielding
the seed within
to the grind

like a streetwalker soiling
the neatly-pressed linen
on countless nameless
shameless beds with
absent wives

those hidden expenses
you offer your favours
and promise excitement
temptation the night sent
with decadent flavours
inspiring the senses
in tasteless safe lives

your companion
though hardly your friend
stands proudly beside you
thoughts white and pure
predictably granular
rightly and whitely
complacently sure
he's innately superior
while you're black and poor

he twists his lips
revolves his hips
and sneers appears
so nice and white
and boy-next-door
so fundamentally
condimentally
safe and sure

anticipating
upon the linen
you crouch there waiting
amidst the crumbs
the idle chatter
and kitchen clatter
a hand reaches over
but passes you by
selecting the other

Death and Birth and In Between

you glance up dismayed
an African maid
her Caucasian brother
your consort for life
yet as sapidly different
as steam and ice
or cats and mice
ineffably different
are salt and spice

On Finding a Photograph of the Poet Aged Seventeen

you
with your black lace
shirt and your twelve-inch
flares and your back-combed
ego you're so bloody
obvious

you
just don't get it do you?
they're not interested in exploring
your depths in case they get out of
theirs they're just paddling
in the shallows

you
won't find it here you know
fumbling in dark corners
at parties with cider-tipsy
anybody's and vacant-staring
nobody else's

you
won't find it there either
with your Saturday night
siren all dimples and Cathy McGowan
hair and eyes you fall into
with a helpless
splash

you
won't even find it next year
up there with the earnest
ones bobbing in the currents of their
cleverness their endless bottles of red
ideals washing down slices of nicely matured
Guevara their wide-eyed astonishment
at the suggestion

you
will discover it
later much later
hiding beneath the surface
in a land full of forests and
lakes you barely know
exists it will creep up on

you
slowly and unnoticed no lightning
flashes or mermaids'
choirs love's invisible
tendrils will wind around your
ankles tightening surreptitiously until
when there is no escape they will slowly pull

you under

story

One of Those Parties

SHE SAT APART FROM THE OTHERS, in an armchair in the corner. She had carefully positioned the lamp so that the top half of her face was in shadow, her scarlet lips the only thing visible. Apart from her naked breasts and the rest of it all, of course. She glanced down nervously – she had shaved for the occasion, not something she usually did, and was conscious of a slight rash. At the last party she had realised that she was the only lady present with hair so had decided to take the plunge. She was surprised to notice that several of the men had done the same.

Everyone was naked, of course. That was one of the rules here, no clothes, although jewellery was allowed. There were all sorts here tonight, all shapes and sizes, colours and ages.

She was nervous and insecure in such settings, so had developed a diffident air to compensate. She just didn't know what to say, had never mastered the art of small talk. could never join in. She hoped that would give her an air of mystery. She hoped too that it made her attractive. Especially to the tall slim black man by the table, who kept throwing glances in her direction. After her divorce she had gone on a strict diet and knew she had recovered the figure of her youth. Maybe that was what he was looking at.

He clearly worked out in the gym, and was well built. Very well-built she thought, her invisible eyes dropping for just an instant before looking up again to his face. So it was true then.

"I hope I get him", she thought. But that was the trouble with this sort of party, you never knew who you were going to end up with.

She took another sip at her wine before glancing around the room. She knew some of them from other visits. Craig, a tall studious looking chap, was glancing around lecherously. She had ended up with him last time. Not bad, but afterwards he couldn't even remember her name. Then there was Simon for whom the conversation afterwards seemed more important than the event itself. She got the feeling he was looking for a route out of his marriage rather than just being here for a good time. And that broke one of the house rules – no commitment, no ties, just fun.

She had first found out about this group from the internet – you can find anything there, she thought. How to build an atom bomb too, she had heard.

"Did the earth move for you?" Crag had said! No really!

She started paying attention when the lottery started, and two by two, like animals boarding the ark, couples shyly stood, took each other's hand and wandered off to the bedrooms. There were only four of them left now. She held one hand in the other to stop it shaking, not wanting her nerves to show. Her number was called, and then another. With a smile the black man who had been eyeing her up wandered over and held out his hand.

"Shall we?" he asked.

One September Day[*]

SOME we saw
toy figures in a doll's house
waving from tiny windowsills before
like migrating birds on a telegraph wire
launching into flight

OTHERS remained hidden
entombed beneath
the smouldering pyre
or consumed instantly
in the dragon's terrible breath

MOST however
were transformed in those moments
when the tallest fell
into dust and ash
rising once more to fall
like unseasonable snow
settling on shoulders and hair
ingraining the pores
invisibly scarring

THE FEW who
running or walking or limping clear
white-shouldered
not yet torn apart by guilt
found themselves the lucky winners
in a sick lottery
someone forgot to tell them
they had entered

story

Patchpuddle

"**MR MOONBEAM?** Mr. Geronimo Moonbeam? Yes, this is PC Shepherdson. We met last Tuesday after the incident on the beanfield. I was the one with the blood pouring from my nose. Yes, you were trying to pull my head off.

"It's about the dog. What was his name? Patchpuddle! Yes, that's it. Well, the court has decided that he is a dangerous animal and will have to be put down . Yes, Patchpuddle. Well, he might be quiet as a lamb with you, but he certainly wasn't last Tuesday, was he? More like a wolf. At times a whole pack of wolves. Ha! Ha!

"The thing is, Mr Moonbeam, that I've … Is that your real name by the way? Now, there's no need to be offensive … Ok, if you say so … We'll use that name for the time being, but the court will need … Now, now, Mr Moonbeam, calm down. What I have been trying to tell you is that I have been ordered to collect him … Yes, that's right, to take him away … Well, to the vets in the first instance. After that he'll, well, we'll arrange for disposal if you wish.

"Well, what did you expect, Mr Moonbeam, after what happened last Tuesday? PC Jackson needed seven stitches in his leg … No, in the confusion of the moment I'm not really sure who bit whom first, Mr. Moonbeam, but Patchpuddle did bite PC Jackson, there's no doubt about that. We have five witnesses. Then he grabbed the truncheon and made off with it somewhere.

By the way, you haven't seen it have you? Jackson was very attached to that truncheon. Had it for years. It had eleven notches on it, one for each time he … What? … Well, where did he bury it? … Yes, I know it's vaguely bone-shaped, but you'd think that even a dog like Patchpuddle would know the difference between a bone and … No, I'm not insulting Patchpuddle … I'm sure he's a lovely dog … Maybe that's true. Maybe last Tuesday wasn't typical, but nevertheless.

"What sort is he, by the way? … Bassetts? I've never heard of that breed … Really! Rare you say!

Death and Birth and In Between

"The strange thing is, Mr Moonbeam ... OK Geronimo ... The strange thing is, when I was a nipper my Aunt Bessie had one that was almost identical. She must have been a Bassetts as well. Wonderful dog she was. Tilly, that was her name. We had many happy hours together ... Yes, Yes, they are very affectionate ... but they do have this unpredictable side to them, you have to admit. One day when I came to visit my Aunt Bessie, Tilly wasn't there any more. Her basket was empty. I cried and cried when they told me.

"The farmer who owned the field next door had shot her! Apparently she'd killed a bull ... No, Tilly, the dog. Bessie was my aunt ... No, she was not a fascist pig too. I mean we are not ... Now, Mr Moonbeam, Geronimo, we really have to discuss the collection of the dog, and sinking to that level of language will not help at all.

"No, there is no other possibility. Well, I suppose there is just the one chance ... That is, if someone else, acceptable to the courts, were to take responsibility for Tilly ... No, sorry, I did mean Patchpuddle ... No, No, it was just a slip, Mr Moonbeam ... Geronimo ...

"Yes, I suppose the courts would consider a policeman to be responsible enough ... No, you don't understand, it's not a question of selling the dog, I have to collect him to take him to the vets ... What? Keep him? Me?

"Well, that is a tempting suggestion, Geronimo ... but I couldn't. I'm not sure it would be allowed, me being involved and all.

"Fifty Pounds, you say ... I see ... You know, I really did love Tilly. I was devastated when they put her down. And angry! I told Aunt Bessie! I said, it's not the dog's fault. You should have taken more care of her. Letting her run free in a field with a prize bull. Asking for trouble, it was.

"Well, Geronimo ... Ok, yes, I think Gerry is less of a mouthful too. Well, Gerry, thinking about your offer, and considering he is such a rare breed and all, I think we might have a deal. Yes, and ten pounds on top for Tilly, I mean Patchpuddle's, lead and muzzle sounds quite fair. I'll pop round this afternoon to collect him.

"In the meanwhile, you see if you can find that truncheon, will you?"

story

Penance

"HOW MUCH FURTHER?" I asked.

He didn't answer, just lowered his head and pulled the paddle more strongly from the shoulder. We had to find it soon. There was not more than an hour's daylight left.

Water lapped from the blade of the paddle as he dipped and pulled, dipped and pulled, with each stroke the boat surging forward, cutting the still water in two.

I would recognise it when we got there, that I was sure of. I had seen the place in my memories and nightmares for the past fifty years. The tree would still be there on the corner of the river, and even if it wasn't, felled by a rogue streak of lightning or toppled through old age, I would know the pool anywhere.

I would feel it.

I peered ahead. It was getting more difficult to see through the gloom. But we were getting near now. I could hear her calling. It wasn't far.

A family of mallards swam out from the overhanging branches on the river bank, mother ahead, youngsters trailing behind. The mother changed direction and led her charge away from the canoe when she noticed our presence. The ducklings followed. They were obedient. They did as they were told. But we had not been. We had disobeyed.

I was eleven the last time I came down to the pool with Gillian, eleven years old. She was nine. It was forbidden, but we came anyway, sneaking away from the wagons, leaving our chores undone. How many times? Four? Five? I don't know. We would crawl into the secret room formed by the huge spreading branches of the willow, and there we would play our game, removing our clothes, each other's clothes, taking turns to look and touch and discover the mysteries that made us different, her and me.

Afterwards we would dive into the water, the cleansing water, and wash our sins away, before returning, unseen and unmissed, to the wagons.

The last time it had been later than usual by the time we finished. And we had taken our explorations and discoveries further than before. We didn't know what we were doing – I was as surprised as her at what happened. But afterwards it was even more important that we dive into the cleansing water for absolution.

Two dived in, but this time the river did not forgive us our sinning ways – this time the river needed penance. Two dived in, but I was alone when I recovered my clothes, alone when I crept back to the wagons.

Fifty years ago.

The rhythm of his paddling changed and I looked up. And recognized. It was smaller than I remembered, the giant willow not a giant at all, the pool no more than a corner cut into the river bend. But it was the place. I was sure.

I got out of the canoe, paid him his money and he left. He didn't question why I had come, why I was here, why I had nothing with me except the clothes I stood up in. He was soon out of sight. For a few seconds more I could hear the dipping of his paddle, but soon even that was gone and I was alone.

I couldn't find our secret room – fifty years had changed the layout of the branches beyond recognition. Maybe it was for the best. I would never know if her clothes were still there where I had buried them.

"I'm here Gillian," I said, and started undressing. I placed my clothes in a neat pile on the bank. The hungry mosquitoes swarmed around me and began to eat me. To feast on my sinful flesh.

"I've come back Gillian. I'm sorry."

I closed my eyes and remembered. We had dived in together, but surfaced apart. I remembered the tug of the icy current on my ankle, her cries for help, and the fear that swept over me when they stopped.

"I'm sorry Gillian."

"Are you sure you haven't seen her," they had asked. "You two are always together. Have you no idea at all?"

But I just shook my head. We had sinned. We had been punished. As they had told us we would be.

Finally I stood up on the bank. The last of the light was fading and a mist was beginning to form just above the water.

It was time. I mustn't hesitate. I had to do it straight away. Otherwise I might not be strong enough.

I dived in and immediately the embrace of the icy water took my breath away. It was time for absolution. The current grabbed my legs in its dull numbing grasp and held on. I had sinned. The river needed penance.

Like an icy hand, the cold water dragged me under.

I have come back, Gillian. I won't leave you again.

Playing Ball

MUMMY WAS PUSHING ME in my pushchair. We were coming home from the shops. As usual she had put the shopping bag in the space underneath my seat. She was wearing her old green and black patterned coat, the one she always wore to the shops, and a headscarf. She always wore that headscarf when she thought her hair was a mess.

She had something on her mind, I could tell. I tried to get her attention in the usual way, by crying a little bit and sniffling a few times, but she just pushed that rubber thing in my mouth and ignored me. She seemed in more of a hurry to get home than usual.

Daddy was out at work. He had left at his usual time. Most days he leaves without any fuss, sometimes even forgetting to kiss us both goodbye. Today, however, Mummy saw him off at the door.

"Dinner at the usual time, Darling?" she said as he was putting on his hat.

"Yes. Got another sodding meeting this afternoon. Hope it won't run over."

"I'll get it for six then. Shepherd's Pie OK?"

But he was already gone.

When we got back from the shops, she put me in my playpen in the nursery and went to her bedroom to get changed. I heard her take a shower, then I heard her using the hairdryer. She took longer than usual, and when she came out her hair was no longer a mess and she had made herself look pretty, with that red stuff on her lips and the blue stuff above her eyes. She didn't know that I could see her, of course. As far as she was concerned, I was quietly playing in the playpen, but I had worked out how to climb out ages ago and was watching through the crack in the door.

There were lots of things I could do that they didn't know about.

She went to the wall cupboard in the kitchen and took out a couple of glasses which she put on the kitchen table. Not our usual daytime gasses, but the ones Daddy called *'for best'*. She took a bottle out of the shopping bag and put it in the fridge, then she spoke to someone I couldn't see.

"Hey Siri, play some romantic music," she said.

And the room was immediately filled with soft gentle sounds. I liked it when she had gentle sounds playing – it made me feel warm inside.

She sat at the kitchen table tapping her fingers and looking at the kitchen clock – the one on the wall that looked like a big red sun. Then she went to the window, opened it and lit a cigarette. Daddy didn't know she still smoked. Whenever he asked, she said she had given up. Eventually I heard a gentle knock on the door. With a glance towards the nursery, she put her cigarette in the ashtray, sprayed something in her mouth then opened the door. A strange man stepped in, someone I had never seen before. He looked as if he wanted to say something, but she put her fingers to his lips, took him by the hand and led him quickly into the kitchen. Then she closed the door.

For a long time, nothing happened. I could hear a gentle murmur of talking, and once I thought I heard a clink of glasses. I couldn't work out what they were saying. Then the kitchen door opened again and Mummy came out leading the strange man by the hand. They went into Mummy and Daddy's bedroom. For a while I couldn't hear anything, but then there was something that sounded like they were struggling. It upset me, I didn't want Mummy struggling with a strange man, and I thought about crying, but decided not to. Then something was squeaking – I think it was the bed – I t sounded like it does when I bounce up and down on it with Daddy. Then it sounded like she was crying out. I didn't like that either and again I thought about crying out myself, but didn't. Then that gentle murmuring again. Then everything was quiet.

I decided to climb back into my playpen and play with my teddies. I wasn't sure what was happening. I think I must have fallen asleep – I usually do about that time in the afternoon – but woke up when I heard the front door closing. Immediately afterwards I heard the sound of Mummy taking another shower.

When she came back into the nursery, she had washed all that stuff off her face and was looking normal again, wearing the same clothes as she had in the morning. The washing machine was going, and I saw that she had changed the sheets from their bed. She had also washed up the glasses and put them back in the cupboard. That surprised me. She had nagged Daddy for ages for a dishwasher. When she finally got one, she refused to wash anything by hand at all. Yet today she had washed up the glasses in the sink. And the ashtray too. There was no sign of the bottle either. She picked me up and kissed me and threw me in the air the way I liked. She gave me much more attention than usual. She seemed really happy.

While she was cooking dinner I crawled to her bedroom. It looked quite normal, with the fresh sheets on the bed and some smelly stuff in the air. Then I noticed something under the bed. It was a brown thing that opened like one of my story books. I opened it. There was money in it, and also a picture of the strange man with a woman I didn't know, together with a child who looked about the same age as me.

I put it back under the bed and crawled out of the bedroom to the kitchen.

Daddy came back at six and they ate their shepherd's pie, giving me that horrible stuff from a jar that had a picture of a baby on it.

"How did you spend your day?" Daddy asked.

"Oh, the usual, shopping and cooking and washing and playing with Gemma."

They both glanced at me.

"You have no idea how much work it all is. I hardly have a moment to myself," she said. There was a pause. And then, "Do you think we ought to take her to see someone?" Mummy asked quietly.

"Why would we do that?"

"She's just had her third birthday, Darling, and she isn't walking yet, and she can't say anything except 'Mama' and 'Dada'."

Daddy went on eating his dinner without looking at her.

"I don't think so. Some children develop faster than others. I'm sure she'll catch up."

I was glad he said that. I was angry with Mummy. I didn't want to be taken to 'see someone'. They didn't know I could understand them, of course, and I didn't let on. Maybe I would have to start speaking properly soon. I was sure I would be able to, I had just never felt the need. And I knew how to walk, of course. It was easy. I just didn't do it when they were around.

After dinner Daddy played ball with me as he liked to do, while Mummy loaded the dishwasher. He rolled the ball to me, then I rolled it back to him. I was getting quite good at it.

Then I had an idea. I hit the ball really hard with my hand. It went through the open bedroom door and rolled under their bed. Daddy said, "Well done Gemma!" Then followed it into the bedroom, bent down and reached under the bed.

*Reflections No 10**
(Tony through the Looking Glass)

Once, like Alice, I stood on tiptoe
Grasped the mantelpiece with both hands
And craned my neck to see if the room
On the other side was indeed the same
But now we have arrived I must say
Those hidden corners
Are not what I expected
And though we achieved the changes planned
The devil's in the detail
Ma Cherie

Rhodri has toed the line so far
But like a walrus on a Welsh beach
He will devour my ideas like clams
Spitting out those he dislikes
To lie discarded in the sand
Alongside the shells

Rather than the March Hare expected
Ken has played the malevolent caterpillar
Crouching on a 1970s mushroom
Smoking his hookah
And telling everybody they have won

Scotland was safe, but then
Who could have foreseen
That my White Rabbit
Would stumble on those steps
That even he would fail me?
Who now can I trust
To lead the story on?

Death and Birth and In Between

At least the backwoodsmen have gone
No longer will they play
Flamingo croquet
Knocking our ambitions back and forth
On their ermine lawn

When I awaken from this dream
Your voices clanging in my ears
Will you remember me fondly
Or with regret?

Will our edifice survive
Or fold like a house of cards
In the first draught of autumn?

Can I ever do more than the Cheshire Cat
And leave a legacy of substance

Instead of just a fading smile?

Remembering Douglas

They overtake you that's the problem
One day a speck in the distance
Chasing seagulls on Holkham beach
Or dementedly greeting the crunch
Of feet on gravel

The next trudging behind
Arthritic but stoic
Tongue hanging out
Eyes fixed as if keeping up
Were a point of honour

But when is the time right?
How can you be sure?

Once he ate an entire chicken
Bones and all
That I left on the side to cool
Do you remember?
And tried to escape
Through the cat flap
When he heard me coming
Legs scrabbling behind
Like a cartoon villain

In the end the local cats
Taunted him as he creaked past
Without even a twitch of nostril or tail

It's so very hard I know
But surely the lights died
In those milky pools
Too long before the vet's needle
Finally flicked the switch

There's an empty hook in the hall
I still reach for
When I walk to the shops

And we'll have to get a doorbell now

story

The Returning Sailor

IN THE YARD THE DOGS were barking. They were huge dogs, black and vicious. But tonight their teeth were bared in fear. I walked slowly past them towards the hut. They could see me. But they couldn't harm me. Nothing could harm me now.

I hadn't realised at first where I was, or why I had been brought back here, to this place, where she'd foundered. But when I looked across the bay, and saw the fires burning on the headland, I knew.

Inside, he was sitting by the fire – a huge blazing fire that I could see had been made using some of her timbers. He had bread and cheese and a jug of ale beside him, and was writing carefully in a large leather-bound book. He dipped his quill into the ink and continued writing. He didn't see me. How could he?

I stood behind him and read over his shoulder. It was an inventory of what he'd stolen. Five ships in the past three months, lured onto these rocks to be wrecked and plundered. Five crews drowned or, if strong enough to survive the waves, their throats slit by his razor.

"Hello Bill," I said.

He whirled round in his seat, his pipe falling to the floor.

"Who's that?"

"You know who it is, Bill. You spoke to me at great length, just two weeks ago. In The Anchor. Surely you remember?"

His eyes were darting from side to side. The red in his cheeks was already fading to grey.

"You were asking me all about the 'Queen of the Seas', when she would be returning, about her cargo. Surely you haven't forgotten? You and your brother, Ted. You were very generous to me that evening, Bill."

"But where are you? I can't..."

"No of course you can't. But you saw me well enough last Friday, didn't you? When I staggered from the water. When you reached out your hand for me. When you put your arm about my shoulders, like a friend. When you took your razor and pulled it across my neck. You saw me well enough then."

"But you can't be, you're…"

The jug fell to the floor, and cracked in two.

"Yes, Bill, I am. And soon, very soon, you will be too. Though I don't think you'll be coming to the same place as me. I think you can feel it reaching for you now, already. Can you Bill? Can you feel it?"

He reached a clawed hand to his throat. A deep croaking sound escaped from his lips.

"And then I'll look for Ted. Is he across the river, Bill? Is there another one due in tonight, is that it? Has he started already, lighting the bonfires, making sure they're just right. Got to be just right, haven't they Bill? Or they won't fool the skippers."

He was sitting back in his chair now clutching his neck, and a deep choking sound was gurgling from his throat.

"And you've got to fool the skippers, haven't you Bill? Or else they won't sail onto the rocks here, and you won't be able to do your work."

He fell onto the floor, ripping at his throat with his fingers, tearing at it, legs thrashing wildly.

"How do you know when it's coming, Bill? How do you know when it's time? Does he signal you? With a lantern maybe? Is that it?"

But then his thrashing stopped, and he lay still on the floor, blood oozing from the wounds at his neck.

I left the hut and walked back through the yard, past the dogs and into the water. As I started swimming I could see, across the river, a light blinking.

The Ring

raising the baby squid to my lips
or was it a sliver of chorizo
skewered on a toothpick
I flinch spilling my Rioja

the cracked ring
pinching my skin like cat's teeth
biting deep into
my swollen finger

not just any ring
one of a pair
fourteen karat gold
once decorated with herringbone

now worn smooth and thin by time
like wedding vows
the jeweller muttering in Spanish
shakes his head in apology

almost tearful before
dividing it in two
then to the seafront for
grilled sardines with black salted olives

and a couple more glasses
of Rioja red as blood
it can be repaired I say
handing the pieces to her

for safe keeping
five years ago
now my naked finger
proclaims to the world

my unmarried state
lying through its teeth
although we two remain
as yet undivided

story

Ripped

IT WAS COLD ON THE MARSH. The wind tore through her flimsy dress like a scalpel. Clouds lay heavy in the sky, and a rumble of thunder together with a flickering on the horizon told her that it was time to head back. The storm would soon be upon her.

As she turned, her dress caught on a bush. She struggled for a moment to free herself, then cursed when it tore slightly. Never mind. She would have plenty of time to mend it at home, peaceful now that he was no longer there. Her hand moved involuntarily and touched the bruise under her left eye. She looked again at the bush and shivered. It was almost as if, even now, he was reaching for her, clutching her, pulling her back.

She felt the first smatterings of rain on her face, and then almost immediately it turned into a deluge. She could see no more than a couple of feet in front of her. No matter. She knew these marshes so well she would have been able to find her way back to the hut blindfold.

Just then a deafening crash of thunder followed almost immediately by a flash of lightening, ripped through the gloom, illuminating the bleak marsh in stark detail.

Before starting back she looked down one last time at the familiar face, no longer red and shouting, but still, cold and expressionless beneath the surface of the marsh waters.

Then with a smile she turned and hurried back. Things would be better now. More peaceful. Quieter.

A Shaggy Dog Story

THERE WAS THE USUAL HUBBUB in the café. Gloria, the waitress, was rushed off her feet. It was always the same when it was raining. There were lorry drivers in for their mugs of tea and bacon sarnies, workmen tucking into a full English, teenagers defying their slim waists with the locally famous apple and blackberry pie topped by a mountain of whipped cream, as well as several table blockers, as Gloria called them, sheltering from the rainstorm outside with just a mug of tea or coffee.

Then the door opened, and he came in, the dog. A large white shaggy Dulux sort of dog. He had a purple collar with trailing purple lead, but no human in tow. He walked to the central passageway between the tables, where everyone could see him, and started shaking. The resonance passed along his body from head to toe, with droplets of water flying in all directions. The hubbub in the room was replaced instantly by a sudden silence. Everyone glared at the dog, who, having finished his shake, gazed placidly back.

The droplets reached everywhere: faces were dripping, Gloria's tights were soaking, and several customers tilted their plates to remove the doggy water bath on their food. But still no one spoke. The dog looked around the room examining each person in turn, making eye-contact and refusing to look away first.

Eventually he strolled up to a businessman who had been eating egg and chips and placed a sodden paw on his knee. The businessman looked into the dog's eyes, picked up the plate and placed it on the floor. The dog gave a brief, almost symbolic, wag of his tail and wolfed it down.

He next went to a workman sitting by the window with an untouched full English breakfast in front of him. He gazed into his eye and placed a paw on his knee with the same result. The workman put the plate on the floor and watched it being devoured hungrily.

The dog licked its lips and gazed around the room again. Still no one had spoken. It was time for dessert. He strolled over to a teenage girl who had a half-finished bowl of pie and cream in front of her. She too placed her food on the floor and it too was quickly demolished.

After all that food the dog was thirsty. He sniffed at each table, examining the drinks one by one, but was clearly not in the mood for coffee, tea or cola, so walked behind the counter, and stared up at Gloria, who poured him out a bowl full of water and placed it on the floor. The dog lapped at the water noisily for a minute or two, then he strolled to the centre of the cafe, walked in a circle three times, dropped down and instantly fell asleep.

The silence in the room continued for several minutes. Then one of the regulars said, "I've never seen anything ..." at which point the dog opened one eye and fixed him with his gaze, and the regular stopped in mid- sentence.

And thus it remained until the door opened again and a man entered. He was spectacularly dressed wearing purple cape, top hat, a neat grey goatee, and an unlikely white boa round his neck. He had a case in his hand bearing the legend *'Alfonse Crabtree, hypnotist'*.

"Has anyone seen my ... oh there you are Genghis, I've been looking everywhere for you." He walked over to the dog and picked up his lead.

He looked around the room apologetically. "I do hope he hasn't been any trouble", he said, "I was starting to panic. I need Genghis for my act, you see, I'm on in fifteen. In the old Hippodrome. Can't go on without him." He shook his head. "It just doesn't work anymore. I don't seem able to put anyone under when Genghis isn't there."

He turned and led the dog towards the door. "Nowadays," he said, "it's almost as if he's the real hypnotist and I'm the assistant."

Then with a dry laugh, Alfonse Crabtree, hypnotist, opened the door to leave the café. At the last moment Genghis stopped at the door and looked over his shoulder, gazing around the room. Then with a single bark, as if to say "Thank you", he too left.

song

Sibelius in the Surf

I came upon a grey land
On a rainy first of May
And now I find it's time to go
I know I'd rather stay

And I hope that my stay here
Means as much to you as me
Friends I'll think of frequently
Though maybe never see

> *And on my far-off island*
> *I'll smell pine upon the breeze*
> *Hear Sibelius in the surf*
> *And paint your faces in the trees*

I leave a green and pleasant land
As May gives birth to June
But something in my heart tells me
It's a lifetime too soon

> *And on my far-off island*
> *I'll smell pine upon the breeze*
> *Hear Sibelius in the surf*
> *And paint your faces in the trees*

I came upon a grey land
On a rainy first of May
And now I find it's time to go
I know I'd rather stay

Siren

  chiming clear
      through discordant
         crashing waves
            no words her
               song no tune
                  trickling notes
                     one after tripping
                        over each other

Why did he go?
    You knew he would have to, my dear
Why didn't he come back?
    Such different worlds, my love
Couldn't he hear my voice?
    Let me comb your hair again
Maybe if I sing just a few minutes more?
    It will calm you

a fire coral fragment
    drawn through tumbling
        onto waterfall hair
            glistening shoulders
                wave-driven spray
                    washes trickles down
                        small rivulets
                          naked breasts

Yes Mother?
    Why do you sit there so?
In case, only in case
    Aren't you cold?
I never feel it nowadays
    The cold?
Not in my body. Not since.

  shaking fanning
    an arc her
      hair bubbling
        seaweed dying
          sunlight a thousand
            tiny rainbows
              catching splintered
                ice fragments

I like this rock, Mother
    Don't stay long my love
Just five minutes more
    It isn't safe
I feel so alive here, where two worlds meet
    Do take care!
Waves breaking on my back
    Take care!!
In the shadow of this cliff
    Your sisters will be missing you soon
If only he might hear my song one more time

    her voice
          discordant surf
              peals through
                    louder one final
                          refrain a lonely
                              harp clashing
                                    cymbals underscore

Mother?
       Hurry my dear hurry!
Yes I know
       They are coming. You must leave!
Yes Mother I know
       There is no time! Can you hear them?
Yes Mother I can

turns headfirst
   dives away pulls
      large strokes her
         finger and thumb webbing
            forcing finally one strong
               flick large green adorned
                  her tail a myriad
                     glistening scales

poem

*Snow**

unexpectedly it came
a real Arctic blizzard
thick snow blown horizontally
not English weather at all

then you
too fast round a corner into a drift
wearing only tee shirt and shorts
you only popped out for cigarettes
after all

you hear your motor cut and die
you wish you'd filled up yesterday
you wish you'd stopped smoking
you wish you'd kept that blanket
on the back seat after all

colder and colder
hour on hour
snow banking up
covering first one window
then the whole car
until there is only darkness
and the taste of fear

just before the end
you fancy you smell cherry blossom
and see pink petals whirling in the wind
and feel a large warm hand in yours
leading you away

song

*Someone I Used to Be**

Here in this place,
With their heavy curtains and their frilly lace,
I seem to be losing life's race,
I feel so old.

I hate this place,
They serve me food I can't swallow
And tea I can't taste,
Too many wrinkles
On everybody's face.
I feel so old.
Won't someone tell me my name?

So I lay here remembering the time
When our hurricanes and spitfires ruled the skies,
In spite of ourselves, we listened every night
To Lord Haw Haw's lies,
When we were young.

Then it was our time,
When we worked on the land
So our boys could go and fight.
Hitler hadn't yet realized
That 20 miles of water
Was his defeat in disguise,
When we were young.

And when I was walking,
All of their heads turned to see.
And when I was talking,
Everyone listened to me.

And when I was laughing,
They all joined in the fun.
And when I was crying,
Offered handkerchiefs, everyone.
I was so beautiful way back then,
When I was young.

>*And I recall,*
>*Someone I used to be,*
>*Someone I used to see, before.*
>*When I stood tall,*
>*And the mirror stared back at me,*
>*Showing someone I liked to see, before.*

Here in this place,
People come and visit I don't recognise.
Things inside my head don't stay the same.
And when I try to speak,
The words just don't come out right,
Someone's in there messing with my brain.

>*And time's undone*
>*All that I used to be,*
>*All that I used to see, before,*
>*When I was young,*
>*And the mirror stared back at me,*
>*Showing someone I liked to see, before.*

I'm lost in time.
The pictures keep on changing, no reason or rhyme.
What's going on with my mind?
I feel so old.

I'm lost in space,
My body and my brain in a different place,
And why's there a tube in my arm
And a mask on my face?

Death and Birth and In Between

I feel so old.
Won't someone tell me my name?

Back then, working the nights on the radar,
Jerry believed us when we said
The reason our boys saw at night
Was because of the carrots they ate
Made the night sky bright,
When we were young.

One night at a dance I saw
A man I'd noticed once or twice before
Watching me, smoking his pipe.
He had easy conversation and a charming smile.
I started to drown in his eyes,
Oh yes, I started to drown in his eyes.
Then he took me in his arms,
Took me close in his arms
And he sang to me.
Oh, how he sang to me.
Oh, how he charmed my soul,
Sinatra was there in my arms,

>   *Someone I used to be,*
>   *Someone I used to see, before.*
>   *When I was young*
>   *And the mirror stared back at me,*
>   *Showing someone I liked to see, before.*

>   *Now I look down,*
>   *On someone I used to be,*
>   *Someone I used to see, before.*
>   *They gather round*
>   *All that remains of me,*
>   *Someone I used to be, before.*

song

*Song for Leila**

When the doctor told us
You were on your way,
We celebrated with a pizza, a peach
And a night at the pictures.
The film we saw was *Superman*
But I'm not a superstitious guy,
The day we first learnt about Leila,
Who we knew was going to be a boy.

Your mother carried you with
Her back held straight, her head held high,
She was so proud, she wanted the world to know
She was going to be a mother.
Pressing all our hands to feel
Your every little kick and move.
This is a song for Leila.
This is a song about birth.

And when the contractions came
Well they weren't so bad at first.
She said they felt just like a warm wave
Rolling up her body.
But later on I could see
That it wasn't such an easy ride.
But each wave's a step nearer Leila,
Another step nearer to life.

Now we come to the final bit
And I'm mopping her brow
And I'm wetting her lips.
She took it so bravely
I had to wipe my tears away.

Now we come to the final push
I see the crown of your head
And she says she thinks she's going to burst.
Then suddenly you're there
And I don't know what to say,
I just blink
And you don't go away.

Then you're in your mother's arms,
Eyes open wide, but you don't cry
You just move your head from side to side,
Looking around,
So brave although so frightened.
I think you've got your mother face
But maybe it's your father's eyes.
I say, "Hello, your name is Leila,
You and me are going to know
each other for a while,"
I say, "Hello, your name is Leila,
And you can call me Dad."

poem

A Spanish River

barren the peak
our rationed mouthfuls sipped
hunting fragments of shade
disturbing lizards

parched-lipped and hasty
our descent an incautious scramble
until first hearing then finding you
springing puzzled from your cradle

beneath a yellow rock
like tears on an infantine shiny cheek
later tinkling laughter as siblings tussle
a rush a pause tumbling

downwards always downwards
in innocent urgency
a high meadow where yellow butterflies
and windblown pink flowers

dance Swan Lake
beside a shrinking snowfield
and quietly there forgotten
an adolescent voyeur

you watch us at rest and play
thinking we are alone
pretending we are young again
a week later

crawling sluggish through
the steaming streets of Madrid
your heavy-lidded eyes first show
no sign of recognition

as you parade in stately elegance
middle-aged portly and self-absorbed
but then a mallard rises startled
and a ripple creases your face

winking at us in recognition
sharing a memory with
an arched eyebrow before
remembering your status

and straightening your collar
you raise your gaze towards the coast
and almost as if the effort is too much
you limp on

song

*The Strand**

What is this strand of hair I find
So long and fair on your lapel?
Its colour neither yours nor mine,
Where did this strand of hair come from,
Do tell?

Whose perfume is it I detect
When, doing the laundry, I smell
The scarf you wore around your neck
Last night? Whose scent could that be dear,
Do tell?

What shadow flits across your brow
Each time you hear St Margaret's bells
Ring out? 'Twas there we swore our vows,
Why do you look so sad?

When travelling on your business trips
In whose arms at night do you dwell?
Whose name is that upon your lips
While dreaming? It's not mine,
I can tell.

What is this hairpin that I find
Under the pillow where it fell?
I wonder have I been so blind,
If I ask you whose is it,
Will you tell?

What's this receipt found in your trouser
Pocket, for the Strand hotel?
That night you worked so late, but now
The fear you lied is a fear
I cannot quell.

Death and Birth and In Between

Those emails you swiftly delete
Are tolling out our love's death knell,
But as you sow so shall you reap,
Tomorrow, dear, maybe farewell.

What will you think if you return
And find me packed and gone, do tell?
Relief or shame? Regret or hurt?
For my part, I just think,
"Go to hell!"

What is this strand of hair I find
So long and fair on your lapel?
Its colour neither yours nor mine,
Where did this strand of hair come from,
Do tell?

While travelling on your business trips
In whose arms at night do you dwell?
Whose name is that upon your lips
While dreaming? It's not mine,
I can tell.

Those emails you swiftly delete
Are tolling out our love's death knell,
But as you sow so shall you reap,
Tomorrow, dear, I'll bid farewell.

What will you think when you return
And find me packed and gone, do tell?
Relief or shame? Regret or hurt?
For my part, I just think,
"Go to hell!"

poem

Strangers

Our eyes met
Our hands met
Our lips met
Our tongues met
Our bodies met

And we were one body
Intensely and utterly
One body

But when the one body
Was again two
There were two sighs
And two tears
And two strangers
Left with nothing

And wondering why

Death and Birth and In Between

poem

Sussex Landscape**

rainclouds glower
over distant hills
a corner turned
a cottage tucked
away in leafy vale
thatched without chimney
wisely you might say
framed by alien trees
a branch snaking like a river
across a counterpane
of ploughed fields

the first of the rain
stings my cheek
before a door opens offering
none too soon
the chance of shelter

story

*Thor's Hammer**

IT WAS COLD, VERY COLD. Not the forgiving domesticated cold of England, but the harsh unrelenting cold of a deep Finnish winter. Underfoot the snow had the unfamiliar texture of hard dry crusted powder, yet overhead there gleamed a bright clear sky, deceptively blue and inviting. It was a day to dress carefully. I was wearing fur-lined winter boots, padded red trousers over long johns, a bright red ski-jacket, thick mittens and a woollen hat. I had rubbed fat into my nose, cheeks and ear lobes to protect against frostbite.

The house was typical for these islands. It was built of logs and painted red with white doors and windows, and stood on a platform of granite. It was empty, yet not entirely still. One of the small panes in a front window was broken, and an old green rocking chair was stirring slightly in the draught.

Britta and I had walked here over the frozen sea from a neighbouring island. Now I was climbing the hill. It was a steep climb, and hard work after the flat trek across the ice. Sweat was running down my face and freezing onto my beard in long icicles. I reached the house before Britta; she had stayed back for a moment and was examining something down by the shoreline.

The door was locked, but I found the small key on its chain where the agent said I would, slotted it into the keyhole and turned. It opened inwards. Its stiff hinges complained at the unaccustomed activity – they needed my shoulder to convince them to give way.

The first thing that struck me was the smell: old wood, old carpets, old musty air, but also, behind that, something else I couldn't identify, something animal. Maybe a fox had found its way in during the autumn and was hibernating in a dark corner somewhere. Do they have foxes in Finland? I made a mental note to ask Britta.

As I started to explore, I could hear a slight creak as the rocking chair continued its stirrings in the unfelt draught. But beyond that there was nothing. No water dripped. No birds sang. No wind blew. Just the slight but insistent creak of the chair.

In the middle of the floor were the decaying remnants of a trapdoor to the cellar. I skirted it carefully and walked through to the kitchen, which was dominated by a huge cast-iron range, and above it a large family of black pots roosting on the hood like ravens. An ancient skeleton of a mouse lay on the table, as if a delicacy presented for our lunch. The kitchen floor had given way underneath one corner. As I walked across the room I found myself veering to the window as if drunk or at sea. I could see the shore from there, and Britta still kneeling by the jetty.

I walked to the door and called to her.

* * *

"It's perfect," she had said as we were walking here across the ice, "Just perfect. Of course, there's a lot of work needs doing."

"Who had the place before?"

"I think he was a seaman," she said. "He built the house. But he died a long time ago – more than thirty years, I think. His wife stayed on for a few years more, but she couldn't take it. It must have been difficult living here through the winter on your own."

We trudged on across the frozen sea, carefully watching for the subtle darkening of the surface that might indicate thin ice.

"One spring they found her wandering around the hillside in her dressing gown, hands and feet almost eaten away by the frost, babbling on about goats. She was in a terrible state. She died before they could get her to hospital."

"Are there goats on the island?"

"No. Some of the other islands have sheep. But we don't keep goats in Finland."

"So the house has been empty for, what, twenty years?" I asked.

"Yes, probably longer."

We walked on for a while in silence, our breath hanging in frozen clouds before our faces.

"Thor's hammer!" she said.

Death and Birth and In Between

Britta was a lecturer in Norse Mythology at Helsinki University, and often punctuated conversations with reference to the 'Old Gods', as she called them.

"What?"

"Weather like this. They used to say it was as hard as Thor's hammer."

We were drawing close to the island now. She took hold of my arm and we stopped walking. We could see the house on the hillside clearly – a flush of red in the otherwise monochrome snow-and-forest winter landscape.

"Perfect, just perfect," she said again.

"Why goats?" I asked.

"What?"

"The old lady. You said she was going on about goats? Why do you think that was?"

"I don't know. I told you, she went mad." She squeezed my arm. "This will be such a fine summer-house. We're going to be so happy here."

"I'll believe you when the snow melts."

"Can't you just picture it? We'll catch fish for dinner. Cut down trees for firewood. You can build a swing for the children. We can hang it from that pine over there. We'll have barbecues, and go sailing and..."

"Children? Woah, hang on there," I said. "Let's have this one first, then we'll talk about more."

The bulge at her waistline was becoming unmistakable nowadays, even when disguised by her winter padding.

"But this place will be just wonderful for children."

"Is there anyone else on the island?"

"No."

"How about electricity?"

"No. But we won't need it in the summer. It's light most of the time, and warm. We can use kerosene lamps when it does get dark."

"No telephone either?"

"No."

"I suppose running water is out of the question?"

"Of course."

She looked at my suspicious expression and laughed.

"There's a well marked on the deeds, we'll be able to find it in the spring. And there's always rainwater. We won't go short. You English – you're so unadventurous!"

"I married you, didn't I?"

She smiled and squeezed my hand. "It'll be wonderful. You wait and see. You'll love it."

We started walking again towards the jetty.

"Take care when we get to the shoreline," she said, "the ice can sometimes be dodgy there. I'll test it first. You walk in my footsteps."

"OK."

She turned to me with a mischievous twinkle in her eyes. "Maybe she was visited by the Gods," she said in a dark voice.

"Who?"

"The old lady. They used to say that Thor travelled round in a bronze chariot drawn by two gigantic goats."

"Britta, don't tease! It was a serious question."

She looked at my expression and laughed. "But really, just look at this place. Can't you picture children running around on the hillside there, or jumping into the sea from that rock?"

But the image that came to mind was of a bearded giant with a Viking helmet, standing in a chariot pulled by a pair of goats the size of stallions, and wielding a gleaming yellow hammer above his head.

"There's even a sauna," she said, and pointed to a small red hut away to our left. "It'll be perfect, just perfect."

* * *

Yet now, looking at the mouse skeleton on the table, the rotten floor, the fragments of ancient lace curtain above the windows, with the pervasive scent of decay clinging to my nostrils, I found myself wondering whether we had made the right decision.

I was feeling cold and slightly light-headed – the musty air in the cottage seemed to be affecting me. I sat down on one of the chairs to clear my head, but stood up again after a few seconds, impatient for Britta to join me. Without her positive chatter I was finding it difficult to build up any enthusiasm.

I noticed a movement out of the corner of my eye. A mouse was sitting on the kitchen table, twitching its whiskers and looking at me, unafraid and curious.

I felt a nagging feeling at the back of my mind, like when a piece of a jigsaw was out of place but you can't work out which one. I turned to the mouse.

"Shouldn't you be hibernating?" I said.

Just then I heard a sound – a new sound behind the creaking of the chair, something high-pitched and distant. I walked back to the window. Britta was still kneeling by the water's edge, bending over something I couldn't make out, hat and gloves discarded on the ice beside her. Her long blonde hair was hanging freely. I had forgotten how beautiful her hair was when it caught the sunlight, the way it shimmered with so many different colours. She glanced over her shoulder towards the house. I smiled and started to wave.

Then I saw her face. It was drained and white, her eyes wide and panic-stricken, her mouth twisted with terror.

Something was wrong! I started for the door, a feeling of dread gripping my stomach. Maybe it was the baby. Maybe she had fallen, injured herself, and needed my help. I shouldn't have walked on up without her. I should have waited. But before I could reach the door a wave of dizziness hit me and I had to sit down again quickly. The air in here was certainly bad – I felt weak and insubstantial. And so very cold.

Death and Birth and In Between

Then I heard the noise again, louder and sharper, and all of a sudden, in a panic, I recognized it for what it was. I staggered back to the window. Britta was standing now. Her mouth was open and her arms were spread wide, as if reaching out to me, to the house, for help. She was screaming.

What I was hearing was the helpless and uncontrolled wail of her desperation.

It was a body. Next to a gash in the ice. Someone had clearly fallen through. But who…? We were alone on the island. I tried to open the door. But my hands couldn't gain purchase on the handle – I was too cold, they were too numb, and the hinges seemed to have locked again. So I returned to the window and looked again at the tableau by the jetty, straining for it to make sense.

The body was unmoving. Dressed in red padded trousers and red ski-jacket. The face underneath the beard was blue and lifeless.

And far too familiar.

I turned away, trying to comprehend, a sense of icy unreality gripping my mind. It couldn't be. It didn't make sense. Who was it, down there on the ice? I tried desperately to remember. What had happened? We walked across the ice. We stopped and looked at the house. She mentioned the sauna – that was the last thing, the sauna. Then…then I was climbing the hillside towards the cottage. What happened in between? Nothing. It was a blank.

I looked up and saw the mouse again, sitting on the table, twitching. That jigsaw piece again. The mouse was sitting where a few minutes earlier I had seen the little skeleton. Or had I? Everything seemed so unreal.

Then I had it. Almost. Like snatching at a dream as you wake up. I remembered turning away from Britta, impatient, and starting towards the hut.

"It looks more like a ruin than a sauna," I had said. "I'm beginning to think we've made a terrible mistake with this place." I took a couple of paces away from her.

"Wait!" she shouted, alarm in her voice. "Don't! It isn't safe!"

Then I turned. That was it, yes, I turned. And stared in amazement at the beautiful shifting mosaic of cracks that suddenly appeared on the ice between us.

I opened my mouth to say something. And then dropped. Into icy numbness.

* * *

The rocking chair in the next room stopped its creaking.

"Welcome," a voice said.

I walked through. Sitting in the chair smiling at me was an old lady. She had matted hair, black teeth, and was wearing something old, torn and filthy that might once have been a pink dressing gown. Her hands and feet were wrapped in tattered bandages.

"Have you worked it out yet?"

I nodded slowly.

"That's good. It's easier that way."

She started rocking again in her chair. "We hoped you would come," she said. "We've waited a long time."

The animal smell I noticed earlier was stronger now. It was seeping up from the cellar through the ruined trapdoor. The old woman looked away from me towards the dark hole in the floor, as if waiting. "It won't be long now," she said. "Listen."

At first I couldn't hear anything, but before long I could make out a rhythmic beating far away, but growing always nearer. At the same time the smell too was becoming more intense. Soon it was strong and pungent, almost overpowering.

It was the smell of goat. Suddenly there was a movement in the foetid air below, a subtle change in the darkness. The beating was loud now, very loud, and I understood what it was, what it had to be. It was the sound of hammer on metal.

She turned to me and smiled again. "It is time! He has come!" She held out her bandaged hand to me and stood up. "Let me take you to meet Him."

poem

Thoughts of a Tin-Opener
on Opening a Tin of Tomato Soup

a sudden flurry of wings as
like a bat
I land on your shoulder

legs coming together
teeth slipping into your neck
like a blade

you twist beneath my iron embrace
and sigh in desperation
but there is no escape

a slight ooze
a hint of red against my lip
then empty

a discarded vessel
as in the candlelight
they gather round to sup

story

To Jenny Joseph[*]

SHE ALWAYS ARRIVED at the poetry workshop wonderfully colour-coordinated. Today, for example, in light-green top, black shorts, green and black scarf and black sandals. Last week in a pink and red combo. Lipstick chosen accordingly. I think she might even adjust her eye-shadow to match, although I didn't want to stare too intently at her eyes in case she got the wrong idea.

It makes me feel like a slob. If my clothes do match it's by accident. My shoes don't see polish from one month to the next, my trousers, or more usually old jeans, worn no matter what shirt I grab from the wardrobe. And my wife is constantly nagging me about wearing white socks.

One day, when the conversation had dried up and, just for something to say really, I complemented her on her dress sense. Mentioned how well the colours matched. Her cheeks reddened slightly and she lowered her head so that I couldn't see her eyes.

"Thank you," she muttered. "But I have always admired your ability to look good in even the most casual outfit that looks as if it has just been thrown together with no thought at all. Very clever."

"I'm not sure clever is the right word," I replied. "Maybe it *has* just been thrown together."

She laughed as if I had cracked a particularly good joke.

"You must have a huge wardrobe," I continued, "to get the effect you do."

"Not that large," she said, "but I keep the items that match together on the same hangers. It saves thought and effort. I know that if I grab a hanger everything on it will work together."

"Are there any colours you avoid?" I asked. She didn't reply, so I kept on talking. "With me, for example, I used to have bright ginger hair, so the one colour I was taught to avoid, from childhood, was red. I always felt it clashed with my hair. Nowadays of course my hair is largely grey, so that no longer applies, but I still think very carefully before I risk anything with red."

"Mauve and purple," she said.

"Why is that?" I asked

"I am too young. I am not sure I won't always think I am too young. But there comes a point when we all have to admit we are not young any more. My mother used to say women should grow old gracefully, but I think that's terrible advice. We should fight it every step of the way. So, for the time being, no! When I am an old woman, I shall wear purple."

"When I am an old woman I shall wear purple," I repeated. "You know, that would make a good first line for a poem. "I paused for a moment, thinking. "You know, maybe you should give people a warning of what's to come, so that they can prepare themselves."

And we both laughed.

poem

*Tony and The Other Place**

The Other Place, stuffed full of musty lords,
Ink barely dry on crumbling vellum, we're
Ordained to sweep those cobwebbed chambers clear
Of velvet dust, and grey unsharpened swords.

Face William's cherub smile, the pompous bore
Attempting to deflect me. This I hate,
But know my wit his ego will deflate
While two sword's lengths apart, here on the floor.

Our victory is in no doubt I ken.
The ayes step left. The nos to right are fewer,
To build our democratic house more pure
The numbers game is played. I win, but then

I realise grim-faced that far too soon,
My seat I'll in the Other Place assume.

song

*Two Sides of the Coin**

When your baby is crying with hunger,
And the milk in your breast has run dry,
Just remember the other side,
Your baby's smile when there's no need to cry.

When the sun in the sky is shining
And the earth is too dry to conceive,
Just remember the other side,
Picture those oceans of rippling wheat.

> *When the head on your coin isn't smiling*
> *And a tear trickles down from its eye,*
> *Just take a quick glance on the other side,*
> *Reach out your hand, you'll find someone to help you by,*
> *Whisper a prayer to the power beyond the sky,*
> *Don't question why.*

When your cow has no pasture to graze on
And the calf in her womb is stillborn,
Just remember the other side,
Soon night is over and then comes the dawn.

When your love has forsaken her suitor
And your letters are written in vain,
Just remember the other side,
Soon you'll be laughing, forgetting your pain.

*When the head on your coin isn't smiling
And a tear trickles down from its eye,
Just take a quick glance on the other side,
Reach out your hand, you'll find someone to help you by,
Whisper a prayer to the power beyond the sky,
Don't question why.*

When your lover returns your embraces
And your pastures are quenched with rain,
Remember the other side,
It's hard to be happy without any pain.

*When your baby is sleeping contentedly,
New-born calves find their first legs with pride,
Just take a quick glance on the other side,
Find a stranger who needs you to help him by,
Just be the answer to somebody's prayer tonight,
Don't question why,*

*For someone will need you,
And someone will cry,
Yes, someone will need you,
Maybe tonight.*

story

The Violin and the Flute

IT WAS ONLY MY THIRD TIME. Online dating that is. The first two had gone extremely well. Everything I'd hoped for. I'd got a taste for it now.

He was a musician, he said. A flautist with the local philharmonic. That was what we had in common. He was extremely keen when I said I too was a classical musician, a violinist. We had arranged to meet at eight o'clock at the Emerald Dragon Thai restaurant. I arrived early, table booked under the name Collins. Not my real name, it goes without saying.

He was late. I hate lateness! I had my violin with me, as agreed, the case on the floor beside my seat. I had taken great care with my make-up and dress. I didn't want to look too remarkable. I liked it when people's eyes slid over me without registering what they had seen.

Eventually a dishevelled man rushed in, tie askew with, I noticed, a slight tear on his trouser cuff. I pursed my lips. He might at least have taken trouble with his appearance. Spotting the violin case, he rushed over to the table muttering apologies. He was, again as agreed, carrying his flute with him.

Both of us seemed embarrassed and uncertain. The evening started with stammered questions and halting responses. Yes, thank you I am well. No, I didn't have to wait too long.

All the time I had one hand on the table and the other hidden in my dress pocket. It was nervously fingering a small bottle. The one I had filled with the distillation from several monkshood blossoms in my greenhouse the day before.

We ordered starters. Spring rolls. Quite tasty really. Then he had Pad Thai and I a vegetarian Green Curry. The conversation was flowing more easily by now. Occasionally we even laughed. Finally, the coffee came.

"I just need to pop to the toilet," he said, coffee untouched on the table. As soon as he left the room, I reached over and discretely poured the contents of the little bottle into his cup. It would taste bitter, I knew that, but then the coffee here was always bitter so I didn't expect him to notice.

As I was replacing the bottle in my pocket and straightening my dress, two men in raincoats entered the restaurant. They did not look as if they were interested in food. Their eyes scanned the room. One of them spoke to a waitress who pointed towards my table.

Shit! I thought. Shit! Shit! Shit! How could they know? Where had I slipped up? Then it dawned on me that I was using the same *modus operandi* for the third time. I had been careful to use different dating sites each time, with different fake personal details. But each time we had met in a restaurant. Someone had sussed it out. Shit! I was calm on the outside but in turmoil inside. How on earth had they tracked me down to this restaurant? Here! Tonight! How had they guessed my next victim? Shit!

Neither of the men in raincoats came towards the table. They just stood by the door, easily able to stop me leaving should they wish, occasionally glancing over at me, waiting. Then my flautist date emerged from the toilets and started walking over. As he did so, I rose from my chair and simultaneously pulled the tablecloth so that everything, including the coffee, fell to the floor. The cup smashed. A futile attempt to destroy the evidence. There were a couple of shouts and turned heads. One of the raincoated men was talking to my date, holding his elbow. He was white-faced. A waiter rushed over apologising and started clearing the mess. The other raincoat man walked towards me carrying the flute case.

"You'd better sit down Miss," he said.

Resigned I sat back down and waited for the inevitable.

"Blind dating is a mugs game," he said. "Really dangerous. But of course, you must know that."

I nodded glumly.

"This man here," he pointed to my date, "has already murdered three women. You would have been his fourth."

He opened the flute case revealing, instead of a flute, a long silver stiletto.

"I suggest you toddle off home and count yourself lucky young lady."

So I did.

story

Was it a Murder?

SHE KNEW IT WAS VALUABLE, possibly Chinese – the word Ming came to mind, but she didn't know what it meant. It was something she had overheard Mummy shouting at Daddy the day before he left. "Why not?" Mummy had said. "You've got enough money for a Ming vase but not enough for me to..." She had tuned them out then. One of their rows was very much like any other.

The vase was blue, ceramic, and showed a constellation, she thought that was the right word, of starlings. Or possibly a murmuration. Or was it a murder? She knew that came in there somewhere. She found these nouns for groups of birds so difficult. They had been doing them in English last week with Mr. Forsythe.

"You're a queer fish, Charlotte," he said to her after the lesson. "In some ways very grown up, extremely intelligent, yet in others," he turned to look out of the window, "still very much a child. Both older than your years, and younger at the same time."

A queer fish. Charlotte didn't really understand that. Daddy had called young Seb Jacobs a queer when he started wearing earrings last winter. But she couldn't see how she was like Seb Jacobs or how either of them was like a fish. There were so many things people said that she didn't understand. But she found she could usually get away with not understanding by just smiling.

"A shoal of fish," Charlotte said, smiling up at Mr. Forsythe.

She was focussing her attention, all her attention, on the vase on the sideboard at the top of the stairs, and the train of thought it had started, so that she didn't have to think about the other thing. She was good at that. Putting things in boxes in her mind, so she didn't have to think about them. In-close-lock and they were gone. Until later when she was alone in bed and she could take them out one-by-one and examine them in peace and quiet.

The other thing, in this case, was the man next to her, who smelt rather bad, to be honest, of whiskey and sweat and something else she couldn't quite put her finger on. She could see Mummy's pearl necklace poking out of his jacket pocket, so had at first thought he must be one of Mummy's friends. Mummy had had so many new friends to visit since Daddy had left, that she couldn't keep up. However, when she bumped into him on the landing in the dark, he had grabbed her and was now holding her arms tightly behind her back, so he couldn't be Mummy's friend then, could he? Mummy's friends generally looked away when they saw her, as if she didn't exist. They didn't twist her arms behind her back so that they hurt. He was also holding a knife to her neck. Mummy's friends didn't do that either. She preferred not to think about the knife. In-close-lock.

She had only got up for a pee. She was wearing her new pink nightdress. "You're a woman nowadays Charlie," Mummy had said, looking her up and down. "Time to get rid of your old jim-jams. This is much more grown-up." She was slightly disappointed, to tell the truth. She quite liked her pyjamas – they had pictures of Winnie-the-Pooh on them, although she had to admit they were getting a bit tight nowadays, especially round her chest. She had thought about taking Mr Teds, her bear, with her to the loo, but decided she was big enough now to leave him on the bed. She hadn't expected to bump into anyone on the way. Which reminded her, she did still need to pee.

"I need to pee" she said.

"Shut up, you stupid bitch," the smelly man growled.

"But I really do!" she continued.

"If you don't shut up I'll..." and he made a sideways motion with his hand across his neck that she didn't understand.

The trouble with pee is that once you start thinking about it, it is impossible to stop it.

"I'm terribly sorry, but...." she said.

Then he was looking down at the fountain of urine that was gushing from her, through her nightdress, over his trousers.

"You filthy little..." he started, grabbing at his trousers and lowering, just for an instant, the knife.

I'm terribly sorry..." she sobbed, "I really am." And then she gave him a push, just a gentle one. Because he really did smell bad. Kippers, she realised. That was the other smell. Kippers.

He took a step back, and she saw him, as if in slow motion, bumping into the sideboard then falling backwards into the void at the top of the stairs. She just managed the grab the vase before it fell off. Then, relieved, she looked back to the man. It was a long flight of stairs, and he bounced a couple of times, still in slow motion, before ending up on Mummy's Afghan rug on the landing below. A pool of something dark was spreading out over the rug. It was coming from his head.

She stared at him for a while, then decided that the dark pool had to be blood and that the man had to be dead. She also realised that if he wasn't one on Mummy's friends, then he had to be a burglar. Why else would he have her necklace?

With a rush of excitement, she realised that they would have to call the police who would probably need to interview her. She imagined Hercule Poirot asking her lots of questions. What would he think? Was it a murder? Or an accident? She *had* pushed him, after all. Suddenly she started to feel frightened. She was worried that some of their questions might be difficult, and she might not know the right answers. She had learned from school that everything had a right answer and if she knew what it was people were happy with her. Something else for later. In-close-lock.

Oh Dear, Mummy will be so angry, she thought. The Afghan is her favourite rug. Mummy would be sure to blame her and start shouting again. Maybe, she thought guiltily, she could pretend it had nothing to do with her at all. Maybe the best thing would be to just go back to bed and close her eyes. Maybe she could pretend she didn't know anything about the smelly man and the blood on the rug.

She tiptoed back to her bedroom, threw her wet nightdress into the dirty linen, dug her old Winnie-the-Pooh pyjamas out and put them on. Then she cuddled up to Mr. Teds, lay there in the dark and listened. The house was quiet. Mummy clearly hadn't woken up at the noise of the fall.

Slowly, one by one, she took those difficult things out of their boxes and started examining them.

"Crows!" she said out loud, giggling, "A murder of crows! That's it!"

Death and Birth and In Between

song

We Came from Babylon[*]
(adapted from *Journey of the Magi* by T.S Eliot)

A cold coming we had of it,
The very worst time of the year
For such a long journey.

A cold coming we had of it,
The weather so sharp and the snow so deep,
It was the very dead of winter.

The camels were stubborn,
Their saddles were sore,
Lying down in the snow by the wayside.
The camel men cursing,
And running away,
And wanting their liquor and women.

It was hard to find shelter,
Our night fires went out,
And the cities and towns were unfriendly.
The villages dirty
And charging too much,
While a voice in my head called it folly.

> We came from Babylon to find a king,
> The ancient prophecy we were fulfilling,
> The bright star in the sky clearly guiding,
> When we left Babylon.

A hard time we had of it.
In the end we travelled at night,
Only sleeping in snatches.

There were times we regretted it,
Leaving behind those silken girls
Bringing sherbet on terraces.

Death and Birth and In Between

Then one dawn we came down
Below the snow line,
And the air smelt of sweet vegetation.
Three trees silhouetted
Upon a low sky,
And we thought that it might be an omen.

We came to a tavern
With vine leaves above,
Where six hands were dicing for silver.
Their feet kicking empty
Wine skins on the floor,
But no news to help us go further.

An ancient white horse
Galloped out of the mist,
And so we decided to follow.
We arrived in the evening
Not a moment too soon,
And it was,
You might say,
Satisfactory.

> *We came from Babylon to find a king.*
> *The ancient prophecy we were fulfilling,*
> *The bright star in the sky clearly guiding,*
> *When we left Babylon.*

All this happened a long time ago,
And yes, I would do it again
Without hesitation.

A sad homecoming we had of it,
It was so hard to explain
What it was we had witnessed.

There was a birth there
Of that I am sure,
But there was a death that day also.
The birth was for us
Hard and bitter like death,
The passing of all we believed in.

We returned to our palaces,
Kingdoms and kin,
But we were no longer at ease there.
With an alien people
Clutching alien gods,
My death, when it comes, will be welcome.

> *We left Babylon to find a king.*
> *The ancient prophecy we were fulfilling,*
> *The bright star in the sky clearly guiding,*
> *When we left Babylon.*
> *When we left Babylon*
> *To find a king.*

song

*We Don't Mean You**

She teaches English at an English university,
Speaks it better than she does her mother tongue,
Owns a house, and is mother to two English girls, and now
A fourth English grandchild has come along,
And I hope when grown, he'll feel that he belongs.

She's lived here thirty years and pays her taxes as you do,
Never claimed a penny benefit on the way.
Did jury service as requested when they asked her to,
And was treasurer of the local PTA.
Yes, she's been a model citizen, you might say.

> *And they say, "My Dear you know we don't mean you.*
> *Yes, you're an EU citizen, but still,*
> *It's the other ones, the ones who take our jobs,*
> *And fill our schools, and steal our homes,*
> *Of these we've had our fill.*
> *But I'm sure you understand we don't mean you."*

And when the vote came through,
And they chose for us to leave,
She was more upset than I have ever seen,
And sad, because this country that she
Thinks of as her home,
Was no longer quite as welcoming as it seemed.
And 'cos some of the things they were saying
Were quite obscene.

When she heard what they were saying
She just didn't understand
Why people wanted to believe the lies
Told by self-serving politicians and the English gutter press,
It seems that tolerance and decency have died.
It's enough to make me hang my head and cry.

And they thought that when they said,
"They should go back where they belong!"
She'd understand it wasn't aimed at her.
And we said, "Of course it won't affect our friendship,"
But it does, 'cos it's so hard
When those you care for cause you hurt.
At times like this you must decide what friendship's worth.

And just how can it be that so much hatred hides unseen?
How come I didn't notice it before?
Like a rotten egg, you look alright
But when I crack your shell,
There's something in there rotten at the core.
I don't think I need to see you anymore.

> *And they say, "My Dear, you know we don't mean you.*
> *Yes, you're European, this we understand.*
> *No, it's the other ones, the ones who take our homes,*
> *Claim benefit and send the money back home*
> *To some foreign land.*
> *But we don't mean you I'm sure you understand."*

There were the gypsies, and the blacks, and the Asians,
And the Irish, and the lesbians and queers,
And the homeless, and the Catholics,
And the Jews and the refugees,
All of these people have, at some time, lived in fear.
Maybe next, European citizens living here.

And after, who'll wait table in the restaurants?
What if the doctors and the nurses all go home?
And who will pick the strawberries
And the apples in the fields?
'Cos you know these jobs we English just don't want.
How will we manage when the immigrants have gone?

And they say, "Of course you know we don't mean you.
You're a foreigner, this we realise.
No, It's the scroungers and the beggars
And the prostitutes and thieves,
It's those other ones, it's them that we despise.
No, we don't mean you, I'm sure you realise."

And when they say, "Of course, we don't mean you."
There's an anger rising in my chest so strong,
Because intolerance and racism and prejudice and hatred
Of foreigners, these things are always wrong,
And that is why I sat and wrote this song.

song

*Woman of Shame**

You wake up in the morning
And your hair is in a mess,
There's make-up on the pillow
And martini on your dress,
And a thousand lip-sticked dog ends
In the ashtray by your side,
And you see that last night's Hercules
Has got acne in the light.

And everything that happened
After twelve is like a dream,
Your memory safely growing dim,
You've forgotten where you put your dignity,
You took it off, when you came in.

So you stumble from the bedroom
While Hercules still snores,
A long dress covers everything,
Don't worry about your drawers.
Take his wallet from his pocket
Trying not to make a sound,
Then take your pill and down the hill
Towards the underground.

The early-morning milkman says
"You're up early love!"
You stop and buy a pint,
and drink it on the spot.
You're surprised to find that you are crying
When you realise just how cheap you've got.

> *Oh you're a woman of shame,*
> *The men they come back again and again,*
> *They use your body*
> *But they don't leave their name,*
> *You give them pleasure,*
> *They leave behind their pain.*

But it didn't have to be that way
You strutted on the childhood stage
The darling of your family and friends.
But what they gave they took away
You had to work so hard to stay
Their favourite, and was it worth it
To achieve your ends?

But it didn't have to be that way
You made your choice, you played their game,
Though never thought that things
Would go so far,
But careless small decisions made
Upset the best-laid plans you made
Unravelling in the back seat of
Your favourite uncle's car.

But it didn't have to be that way
They didn't make you walk away
When you discovered what grew there inside,
But things like that you couldn't say
The shame you felt, the trust betrayed
You vanished rather than remain
Behind and have to lie.

> *Oh you're a woman of shame,*
> *The men they come back again and again,*
> *They use your body*
> *But they don't leave their name,*
> *You give them pleasure,*
> *They leave behind their pain*

You awaken from your reveries,
Tears streaming down your face,
A bowler hat beside you
Offers you his handkerchief.
He offers you a coffee too,
You feel you want to run
But you haven't got the guts
And so you say, "That sounds like fun."

And you realise just where it will lead you,
Right back into bed,
It's the last twist of the knife,
But it's the only way you know
To make a living,
You'll soil his sheets,
But he will not share his life.

> *Oh you're a woman of shame*
> *The men they come back again and again*
> *They use your body,*
> *But they don't leave their name*
> *You give them pleasure*
> *They leave behind their pain*
> *You take on all their pain.*

Notes

Across the Fields The first line of this story is taken from the Philip Larkin poem *There is an Evening Coming In*.

And What has Time? We lived in Jeddah in Saudi Arabia between 1979 and 1986. It was difficult to get married status contracts there, so most of my ex-pat friends and colleagues were single men, and many of them were gay. This period saw the beginnings of the AIDS epidemic among the worldwide gay community, called at that time GRID (Gay Related Immune Deficiency). Towards the end of our time there, several of my gay friends left suddenly without explanation. We later discovered that they had become sick.

This song was inspired by that situation, how it might feel to suspect you have AIDS, waiting for test results, waiting for symptoms to appear and regretting past behaviour.

A recording can be found on the album *Someone I Used to Be.*

Archipelago Days Between 1981 and 1998 we had a bungalow on land owned by Malle's parents on the island of *Kalvholm*, near to *Korpoo*, in the Finnish archipelago between Finland and Sweden. Unfortunately, when they became too old to maintain the property, it was sold.

This song describes the simple yet idyllic summers we spent there and the sense of loss we felt when it was sold.

A recording of this song can be found on the album *Follow Me!*

Birth My first attempt at a sonnet. When I read it during an early visit to Norwich's Writer's Circle, the organiser virtually accused me of plagiarism, which is a kind of back-handed compliment, I suppose.

Catherine Hickman A protest song! In 2018 I watched a TV documentary entitled *Fires that Foretold Grenfell* which is where I first heard about Catherine Hickman. Much of the information in this song I learned from that programme, the rest from online accounts of her inquest.

A recording of the song can be found on the album *In Aleppo*.

Coffee and Cream Mixed-race relationships are commonplace nowadays, but not so long ago the racism that was endemic in this country made such relationships very difficult. This poem imagines one such relationship in conservative rural Norfolk.

The Cruel Incarceration of Pauline Sheldon This is an attempt to write a poem in the style of Edgar Allan Poe.

Pauline Sheldon is the name of a girl I was infatuated with at university but who showed only fleeting interest in me. I am eternally grateful to her, however, as it was her enthusiastic tales about an idyllic summer in Finland which inspired me to travel there myself, and it was there that I met Malle, my wife of nearly 50 years. So, on reflection, her fate in this poem is maybe unwarranted!

The Dragon's Breath I have always been fascinated by the lost underground stations of London. *Down Street* is but one of many! The facts I have included, such as the relocation to the station of Churchill's war cabinet, the frequency of trains and the number of steps down to platform level, are correct to the best of my knowledge. The layout at platform level back then, however, is pure invention.

The Dream If God were to visit me in a dream, I am sure I would be far more likely to listen to his (her?) message if he visited in the form of someone I know and trust, such as my mother, rather than a scary warrior.

Flotsam In this story I explore how appearances can be deceptive. When describing the young man, I was picturing my daughter Tina's partner, Rich, who told me once that, because of his dreadlocked appearance, he frequently had people coming up to him asking to buy drugs.

Follow Me In some ways, at least at the personal level, this is the most important song I have ever written. In 1973, after spending a wonderful summer with Malle, hitch-hiking in Europe, I left for a two-year stint in Grenada with VSO, while she returned to school in Finland. Before parting she asked me whether I thought we had any prospects of a future together. As we were going to be living on opposite sides of the world for a couple of years, I didn't see how we could, so replied with some bland comment like "Let's see how we feel when I get back". After a few weeks in Grenada, however, I found myself missing her intensely, so I wrote her a letter – in those pre-email days it took a couple of weeks to get a reply – which she quite rightly ignored, as she did the next one. So I wrote this song, recorded it on a cassette player in my bedroom, with the sounds of dogs barking and cocks crowing in the background, and send it to her. That did get a response! She came out to live with me the following summer and we married a year later.

This song is available of the album *Follow Me*.

Fool's Gold All my life I have been struggling to reconcile my desire for religious certainty with my education as a scientist.

This song can be found on the album *In Aleppo*.

For Us A love song that took me 50 years to finish! I started it in Grenada in 1973, but could never find a continuation I was happy with. Finally this year, in 2023, I managed to complete it using a completely different melody.

Golden Slippers When I first travelled to Morocco in the mid-nineties (described in my book *Steel Wheels to Marrakesh*) I visited the old slave market in Marrakesh and was shocked to discover that the trans-Saharan slave trade was not abolished by the French colonial authorities until 1923, and that slavery itself continued in Morocco well into the 20th century. It occurred to me then that it was quite possible for children who were sold into slavery in the early years of the century to still be alive.

Hotel Room This poem was inspired by the painting of the same name by Edward Hopper.

In Aleppo I was trying to explore, in song, what it might be like to be a child in a war zone. Then, all by itself, the song changed direction entirely and ended up somewhere totally different.

A recording of this song can be found on the album of the same name.

In Broad Daylight Inspired by the ordeal of the 104 foreign hostages who were kidnapped in Beirut between 1982 and 1992, the most famous of which were Terry Waite and John McCarthy.

Death and Birth and In Between

In Neptune's Bed. Once I saw a woman walking out into the sea fully dressed with apparently no intention of stopping. This song is her story, written long before I learned about the lost town on Dunwich on the Suffolk coast., where the last of the churches vanished beneath the waves a little over a hundred years ago.

A recording is available on the album *Someone I Used to Be.*

It's Still There When I first visited Thailand in the 90s, the beaches were pristine. On recent visits, however, I have seen an increasing amount of plastic washed up on the shore. Thailand is not alone in this, of course.

A recording of this song can be found on the album *In Aleppo.*

Joseph Stanley My great grandfather was a black West-Indian sailor who landed in Liverpool, probably in the 1870s, and married a white woman. This song is, to the best of my ability and the information available to me, a reconstruction of his story.

A recording of it can be found on the album *Follow Me!*

Krunchy's Final Gig A recording of this song can be found on the album *In Aleppo.*

Last Xmas Krampus is indeed a mythical horned figure who assists Santa on his travels, scaring and punishing children that have misbehaved. I have used artistic licence to relocate the character from Alpine folklore to Lapland.

The Morning After A recording of this song can be found on the album *Someone I Used to Be.*

My Dylanesque Song A friend and I were arguing about who was the better poet, Bob Dylan or Leonard Cohen. I favoured Cohen and said that many of Dylan's songs are just doggerel, and that I could write a song in the style of Bob Dylan in an hour. This is it (although it took me a couple of hours).

A recording is available on *In Aleppo.*

Nobody Sees One of my earliest pieces. Passing through Waterloo station late one evening when I was a student, (fifty-odd years ago!) I saw two policemen manhandling a tramp out of the station. I recorded this song twice so it appears on the album *Someone I Used to be* and also together with Malle on *In Aleppo*.

Not a Love Song While on holiday in Thailand a few years ago, Malle asked me why I had never written her a love song. I made some glib comment about there being far too many love songs already. I saw that she was disappointed however, so sat and wrote this in the hotel room after she went to bed. It was startling how easily it came, as if the song had been waiting there all along and I only had to start writing to discover it.

There is a recording of the song on the album *In Aleppo*.

One September Day Everyone can remember where they were when they first heard about, or saw TV footage of, the planes flying into the twin towers of the World Trade Centre on September 11th 2001.

Reflections No 10 Written during the early years of Tony Blair's first government in the late nineties. For those readers who are not as old as me, I will explain some of the references.

Cherie Blair is Tony Blair's wife. *Rhodri Morgan* became First Minister of Wales in 2000 and held the post for nearly ten years. The *White Rabbit* is *Donald Dewer* who was First Minister of Scotland after devolution from 1999 to 2000 when died in office after a fall led to a fatal brain haemorrhage. *Ken Livingstone* was the first Mayor of London from 2000 to 2008. The *backwoodsmen* were the hereditary tory peers who could block legislation in the House of Lords and whose right to vote was removed in the House of Lords Reform Act 1999.

Snow In January 1987 heavy snow fell in the East of England. Road and rail connections were blocked by snow and Norwich was cut off for a few days. Motorists were trapped in their cars. I remember one account of a driver freezing to death in his car wearing only tee shirt and shorts.

Someone I Used to Be My mother died with dementia. Towards the end she lost track of who, where and even when she was. I felt that her mind was drifting back to times when she was happier. As a teenager during World War II, she worked in the land army before becoming a radar operator. At the end of the war, she was stationed in Italy and joined *Stars in Battledress,* a group of entertainers from the armed forces who put on shows for servicemen. She was a tap dancer and it was in one show that she met my father, a singer who sang in the style of Frank Sinatra.

A recording of this song can be found in the album of the same name.

Song for Leila I wrote this song in the days following the birth of our oldest daughter Leila in August 1979. Although it was unusual for fathers to be present in the delivery room at that time in the UK, Leila was born in more progressive Finland where it was encouraged.

There is a recording of it on *Someone I Used to Be*.

The Strand There is a recording of this song on the album *In Aleppo*. Malle insists it was inspired by the TV programme *Doctor Foster*, though I wasn't aware of it at the time.

Sussex Landscape This poem was inspired by a woodcut of the same name by *Eric Ravilious*.

Thor's Hammer Malle and I did actually walk across the ice as described in the story, on one of the coldest days of a particularly hard winter. Afterwards we were told by neighbours that we were fortunate as we had walked over a place where there was a current and the ice was usually thin.

To Jenny Joseph One of my favourite poems is *Warning* by *Jenny Joseph*, which begins with the line *When I am an old woman I shall wear purple*. I decided to write a piece which ends with this line.

Tony and The Other Place This poem was written during Tony Blair's first government during which the House of Lords Act 1999 was passed, drastically reducing the number of hereditary peers and increasing the number of life peers. The leader of the conservative opposition at the time was William Haig.

Two Sides of the Coin A recording of this song can be found on the album *Someone I Used to be*.

We Came From Babylon I was trying to write a Xmas song describing the birth of Jesus from the point of view of one of the other participants. In the end I realised that *T.S. Eliot*, in his *Journey of the Magi* had done it far better than I ever could, so I instead I set his poem to music and added a chorus.

A recording can be found on the album *Follow Me*.

We Don't Mean You Shortly before the fateful Brexit vote in 2016, we were visiting friends for dinner. They were denigrating EU immigrants without seeming to realise that Malle was herself an EU immigrant. The day after the vote, she was deeply unhappy, saying that for the first time she had been made to feel unwelcome in this country. I posted her comments of Facebook. A couple of hours later we received an email from those friends stating, "We Don't Mean You!"

A recording can be found on the album *In Aleppo*.

Woman of Shame Another old piece. Making my way home from an all-night party in London when I was a student, I saw a woman running down the hill looking fearfully over her shoulder. She bought and drank a pint of milk from a milkman then vanished into the northern Line. This is my imagining of her story.

A recording is available on *Someone I Used to Be*.

ABOUT THE AUTHOR

Colin Payne is a retired secondary school teacher and university lecturer, sometimes of English as a Foreign Language in Sweden, Finland and Saudi Arabia, and sometimes of Mathematics in Grenada and England.

He graduated with a BSc (hons) in Mathematics with Aeronautics in 1972 from Southampton University and an MA in Pure and Applied Linguistics from the New University of Ulster in 1979.

Colin is married with two children and four grandchildren.

Colin has written a travel memoir, *Steel Wheels to Marrakesh* and a chess openings book *The Vienna Gambit for the Club Player,* both available from Amazon.

He has recorded three albums of his own songs, *Someone I Used to Be* 1992, to be rereleased in 2023, *In Aleppo* 2019 and *Follow Me* release planned for 2024. These are (or soon will be) available through streaming services such as Spotify, Apple Music, YouTube, etc.

AUTHOR'S NOTE

The recordings of my songs can be found under the name *Colin R Payne*, should you choose to look for them, (and I thoroughly recommend that you do!) The reason being, would you believe it, there is also at least one recording by someone else with the name *Colin Payne*.

There is also a novelist with the same name writing in the UK, (though I am sure, judging by this bio photograph, that I had the name first!) However, as I have never written a novel and have no intention of ever doing so, there should be little chance of confusion.

Clearly my name is more common than I thought!

Death and Birth and In Between

Printed in Great Britain
by Amazon